By Lynne Sella

THE DEPUTY SARAH MURDOCK SERIES

Grave Robber

Snake Charmer

Horse Wrangler

Gold Digger

BETWEEN THE CRIMES BOOKS

A Picture Perfect Romance

GOLD DIGGER

Lynne Sella

WingSpan Press

Published in the United States and the United Kingdom
by WingSpan Press, Livermore, CA

The WingSpan name, logo and colophon are the trademarks of
WingSpan Publishing.

ISBN 978-1-63683-049-0 (pbk.)
ISBN 978-1-63683-961-5 (ebk.)

First edition 2023

Printed in the United States of America

www.wingspanpress.com

This book is dedicated to my mother, Katherine Baker, who was my number one fan and a huge supporter of my writing career.

Thanks, Mom

ACKNOWLEDGEMENTS

This book is a recognition of the beginnings of this series in its format and welcomes the return of several previous characters. Initially started in November 2019 during NaNoWriMo (National Novel Writing Month), it took much longer to complete than expected, and I am again indebted to several people who helped me along the way. A huge thanks to my own personal medical team (and twin daughters), Katie Anderson and Sarah Sella-Hubbard who were always willing to answer my numerous questions about medical procedures and conditions. I would also like to thank Deputy Bryan Sullivan of the Lassen County Sheriff's Office who provided insight to department procedures and policies. And continuous thanks to friends Mike and Lindee Larsen, my resident experts on all things pertaining to life in Surprise Valley. Most of all, I would like to acknowledge my loyal fans who have patiently waited for this next book in the Deputy Sarah Murdock series. Thank you!

GOLD DIGGER

CHAPTER 1

"Why do I have to do it?" he demanded.

"Because you're the stupid son-of-a-bitch that blabbed about having all that cash," his uncle said.

"You realize you just called your own sister a bitch." He grinned. "Don't think she'd appreciate that."

His uncle whipped off his ball cap and smacked the young man on the head. "You know what I mean. Now get going before you lose sight of him. I don't care what you have to do, just don't come back without it."

The bell tinkled against the glass door as Remy Hamilton and I pushed through the door of the Wagon Wheel Café, announcing our arrival. The only one remotely interested was the waitress, Sal. She looked up immediately but was clearly disappointed when she realized who it was. Sitting in our usual spots at the low, pink and green Formica counter, we waited to place our order.

Sal finished her round of coffee refills, returned the pot to its warmer, and started down the counter. She'd almost reached us when the cook tossed two plates of food on the shelf of the pass-through, slapped the bell a couple of times and yelled, "Order up."

The waitress backed up, grabbed the plates, and headed toward the people sitting closest to the door. The man and woman seated there shook their heads as the food was placed on the table. A brief disagreement ensued until the couple in the adjoining booth interrupted and the order was moved to its correct location. That settled, Sal returned to the counter. Pulling an order pad out of the pocket of her pink waitress uniform and a pen from the brassy blond hair piled on her head, she asked, "What'll it be?"

"Is that liver and onions I smell?" Remy asked. After a fairly long pause, he repeated the question.

"Huh? Oh, sorry. Yeah, that's our special today." Again, her gaze was drawn to the front door.

"I'll have that and a cup of coffee."

When she didn't acknowledge him, I said, "Sal?"

"What?" she muttered, still focused on the door.

"Are you all right?" I asked. "You seem a little distracted."

"Me?" She stared at me for a moment. "Oh sure, sure. I'm fine." She began writing something on her pad. "You say you wanted the meatloaf?" she asked Remy.

He shook his head. "Liver and onions, extra crispy, with fried taters. And you can skip the salad."

"I'll take the meatloaf," I interjected before she had a chance to alter the ticket. "Baked potato and I'll have the salad. Blue cheese dressing."

Sal quickly scribbled down the order. "And to drink, Hon?"

"Water will be just fine, thanks."

She tore the ticket off her pad as she moved away and clipped it onto the circular ticket holder hanging over the pass-through window. Then she returned with my water, the coffee pot and an empty cup. As she began filling it for Remy, another tinkling of the bell against the glass alerted us that someone else had entered the café. This was followed by a loud shriek from Sal just as the liquid she was pouring reached the brim of Remy's cup and overflowed onto the counter. Unaware of the mess she'd made, she put down the pot and rushed toward the door. "Oh Henry, I'm so glad to see you!" she exclaimed as she threw her arms around the man's neck.

"That there's quite a welcome, Sally." He, in turn, grabbed her by the waist and twirled her around.

I pulled a handful of napkins out of the metal dispenser and handed them to Remy. "Do you know who that is?" I asked as we watched the energetic exchange.

"Can't say as I recognize him," he said, mopping up the puddle of coffee.

"If I had to guess, I'd say he's the reason Sal has been so preoccupied."

"Uh-huh."

"Come on over here and sit down." Sal led the man to a spot at the counter a few seats away from us. "Are you hungry? What can I get you?" She stepped back around to the other side, handed him a menu and waited, smiling at him the entire time.

The man was at least three inches shorter than Sal and had salt and pepper hair that nearly touched his shoulders. The bushy eyebrows and scraggly beard covering the lower half of his face gave him the appearance of a mountain man. His slight build was hidden beneath baggy pants and a wool shirt worn open over a less than spotless T-shirt.

As she waited for the newcomer to decide, Sal caught the two of us staring. "Oh for heaven's sake, where are my manners? Henry, these folks are two of my regulars," she said as she nodded our way. "This is Remy and Sarah is our resident Deputy Sheriff."

"Most folks call me Haywire," Henry said, nodding at us.

"What brings you to Surprise Valley?" I asked.

"Why, he came to see me!" Sal exclaimed.

"That so?" Remy said. "Well, nice to meet you, Haywire."

"Right back at ya." Closing the menu, he added, "I believe I'll have me that ribeye steak with mashed potatoes."

"Sure thing," Sal said, still smiling, "and to drink?"

"A beer would be nice..." Sal shook her head. "But since that's not an option, how about a cup of coffee. It'll help keep me warm on this chilly evening." Sal turned in the order, filled his cup with fresh coffee, and then sat in the seat next to him. "At least until I get the truck unloaded and a fire started."

"Do you own property around here?" I asked.

"Not exactly. I'm part-owner of a mining claim up Highgrade Road, and I stay in the cabin up there."

"He shows up about this time every year to make a withdrawal," Sal said. "Isn't that right, Hon?"

Henry let out a nervous laugh. "That's a good one—make a withdrawal."

"But are you sure you want to go up there tonight?" she asked. "It's almost dark and supposed to get real cold."

"I need to unload the truck and get things situated. I may be here a while depending on how the prospecting goes." Noticing Sal's expression, he added, "But I'll come down first thing in the morning for breakfast. How's that sound?"

Sal's smile made her look ten years younger. "Just fine." She got to her feet and moved to the other side of the counter. "I'll make sure Cookie whips up a fresh batch of sausage gravy, too." She grabbed the coffee pot and made another round of refills, starting with Remy, and this time the coffee stayed in the cup.

Hoping our dinner would be up soon, I leaned my

elbow on the counter and turned toward Remy. Neighbor and self-proclaimed partner during several of my investigations as deputy sheriff, he had convinced me to try his new hobby, but I had reservations on the outcome. "Still don't think this is a good idea," I whispered. "I've never done this kind of thing before."

"Relax," Remy said. "It's not that difficult, and there's always someone willing to show you what to do. I've been doing this for two years and still don't know how to do everything."

"And what about the equipment? I don't have..." That's when I realized Sal was standing in front of us, her eyes as big as the plates she was holding and her mouth wide open. "Something wrong?" I asked, sitting back in my seat in order to make room on the counter.

"I don't...I mean...what are you..."

"Knitting," Remy said, grinning through his white beard.

"What?" Sal looked even more confused.

"I'm taking Sarah here over to knitting class at the Mountain Weavers."

"Ohh," she sighed and then chuckled as she set down our dinner. "You had me going there for a minute. I thought you were talking about—well, never mind what I thought. Need anything else?"

"Mustard and then I think we're set," Remy said.

"Coming right up."

Remy drove to the south end of Main, turned left across the wide street, and parked in front of an odd-looking white building located next to the firehall. We'd almost reached the front door when he suddenly stopped. "Oh hell's bells, I've left my bag in the Land Cruiser. Go on ahead. I'll grab it and catch up to you."

Still unsure of how successful the evening was going to be, I pulled open the door, passed through a small foyer, and entered the store. Skeins of yarn in every imaginable color were stuffed into boxes laid on their sides and stacked four or five high around most of the room's perimeter. Glass cases held handmade jewelry and pottery as colorful as the yarn. Knitted scarves, hats, sweaters and placemats as well as woven shawls, rugs, and saddle blankets were displayed throughout the store. But most impressive were the looms of various sizes which dominated the back corner. I was moving closer to investigate when I heard Remy call my name. "In here," I answered.

He stuck his head in the doorway. "What are you doing?"

"Are you sure we're here on the correct day?" I asked. "No one is around."

"Not here—upstairs."

With one last look around, I stepped back into the foyer where Remy opened a door I hadn't even noticed and led the way up a narrow, steep stairway. As we approached the top, I heard voices.

"There you are," someone said as we entered the huge, open room that encompassed the entire second story. A tall, thin woman a few years younger than Remy walked around the large table that sat in the center of the room and approached us. "We were beginning to wonder if you were going to make it."

"Wouldn't miss it," he said, slipping past her and moving toward the far side of the table.

"I see you've brought along someone new." She stepped closer and held out her hand. "Robin Byrd."

As in a robin is a bird? "Sarah Murdock," I said, completing the handshake.

"I know what you're thinking, robin—bird, but when

you're in love, you don't always think things through. Thank goodness my husband's last name wasn't Redbreast."

That got a chuckle from the others sitting around the table, most of whom I recognized.

"Let me introduce you," Robin said. "We have Mabel Swanson."

"Good to see you," the middle-aged woman said, peering at me over her readers. I recognized her as a witness I'd met during a recent investigation, mostly because of her grey and black hair wound into a bun and secured with a tie that matched her oversized sweater.

Robin continued around the table. "Abigail Flowers."

The petite owner of the High Desert Hot Springs removed her reading glasses and said, "Why hello, Dear."

"Bonnie Patterson."

"Hi, Sarah." The Bureau of Land Management biologist was out of uniform, wearing instead a pair of jeans and a sweatshirt decorated with wild horses.

"Nice shirt," I said.

She smiled in return, acknowledging our private joke.

"Herb Leibowitz."

The slight man's hair was thinner, but he seemed more relaxed than the last time I'd seen him at the convalescent hospital. He'd traded his horn-rimmed glasses for a more trendy translucent frame and his suit and tie for jeans and a light, tan-colored sweater over a button down shirt. "Nice to see you again, Deputy."

"Shellie Greer."

The part-time bartender from the Silver Spur Saloon had traded her usual ankle-length skirt and sandals for wool pants and boots, but the hint of patchouli was still there. "So glad you agreed to come. Remy was so hoping you would," she said, smiling at the man with whom she'd become more familiar over the last few months.

"Marjorie Callaghan."

"Evening, young woman." A force to be reckoned with in person or behind the wheel of her metallic pink Cadillac, she was also a woman of many surprises.

"And Eloise Borden."

"Hello," the small woman said quietly. She pulled her cardigan, which was perfectly color-coordinated with her floral dress, tighter around her shoulders. "I'm here with Marjorie because she insists my home in Eagleville is too far away for me to drive alone in the dark." Recalling bits and pieces of previous encounters I'd had with Mrs. Callaghan, I knew exactly who Eloise was.

I found a place to sit next to Remy who was already pulling balls of yarn and knitting needles out of a large bag whose material—fall-colored leaves on a dark blue background— reminded me of a sofa my parents used to have.

He grinned at me. "Peg's crochet bag. Thought it was perfect to carry my knitting."

The longer I knew Remy, the more I learned about his deceased wife. A fantastic cook, Peggy Hamilton was also a collector of chicken inspired decorations as well as the animals themselves and a meticulous housekeeper who apparently enjoyed crochet.

"Are you a novice knitter?" Robin asked.

"Oh most definitely," I replied. "No clue how to even begin."

"Well, you'll need a set of knitting needles..."

Without missing a beat, Remy handed over one of the pairs he'd brought.

"...and some practice yarn," Robin said. "I have several balls to choose from." She retrieved a box from one of the many pew-like benches lining the walls of the room. "All these have been knitted and unraveled too many times to count.

"The first thing you'll need to learn is how to cast stitches onto the needle." Robin picked up the ball of dark brown yarn I'd selected. "Let's say you're going to make a five-inch scarf. Using the method I'm about to show you, you'll need about three times that to begin." She pulled 15 inches of yarn off the ball. "Next, you will need to make a slip knot to get it onto the needle." She demonstrated how to form a loop and pull the yarn up through the middle a few times and then handed it to me.

As I took the yarn, the quiet chatter of conversation stopped. I looked up and found myself the center of attention. Everyone was watching to see how I'd do. *Oh, no pressure there!* It only took two tries, and I had a slipknot. No applause but lots a smiles around the table.

"Slide that onto the needle, pull on both sides to tighten the knot, and we can go on from there." After it was nice and snug on the needle, Robin took it back and continued her instructions. "To cast on, slide the knot toward the end of the needle and hold it in position with your right index finger. Then take hold of the yarn with the fingers of your left hand, keeping your thumb pointing up," she said, showing me how to hold it. "Now sweep your thumb behind the yarn so you have a loop around its base. Then poke the point of the needle into the loop from the bottom and grip the needle with your left hand. Take the yarn coming from the ball with your right hand and bring it around the back of the needle and between it and your thumb, keeping it taut. Last, you slip the loop off your thumb and onto the needle." She repeated her demonstration two more times and then handed it over. Talking me through the motions, I was able to add two more cast on stitches. "Now, try adding more on your own," she said.

Slowly, I continued to put more stitches on the needle until only a short piece of yarn remained in my left hand.

Robin inspected my handiwork. "Not bad," she said. Then, before I could stop her, she pulled the needle free, took hold of both ends of the yarn and unraveled every one of the stitches. "Now," she began, handing it back to me, "do it all by yourself. If you can't start a project, you can't knit a thing."

So, I started over and somehow miraculously formed the slip knot and slid it into place. Then, slowly and with lots of coaching, I got all the stitches back onto the needle.

"Fantastic," Robin said. "Unravel it and do it again." More smiles around the table indicated they understood the torment of being a novice knitter.

As I became more proficient at the task, I began to pay more attention to what was going on around me. Conversations covered troubles between neighbors, strangers spotted passing through the valley, domestic disputes, and upcoming births and nuptials. It was a wealth of intel. *I've struck the motherlode!*

"Still have second thoughts about knitting class?" Remy asked later on the way home.

"Nope," I replied.

"Think you'll wanna go again?"

"Sure thing. I think I'll learn a lot."

"I'm sure you will. Robin is a great instructor."

Not exactly what I meant, but I'll go with it. "I even saw a saddle blanket that will look great on Raven. Think I'll get it next time."

"Well, alrighty then. A good night all around."

I slouched down in my seat and closed my eyes. "Sure was."

"And I'll even bet you actually get to knit next time."

I was just drifting off to sleep when Remy said, "Wouldja look at that."

"What?" I asked.

"It's snowing."

I sat up and looked through the windshield. Large snowflakes illuminated by the headlights slowly drifted down onto the ground in front of us. "Looks like winter has arrived."

CHAPTER 2

He knocked a third time and still no one came to the door. Taking advantage of the situation, he made his way around the building, trying every door and window he came upon, but it was locked up tight. The young man shivered; he needed to get inside. Then he remembered something and walked back toward the road until he reached the homemade signpost he'd noticed on the way in. Besides the Big House he'd just been to, there was a sign for the Barn Yard, a shop of some kind, and an Other House. Heading in the direction of the arrow, he followed a trail through the property toward a small building he could just make out in the darkness. Repeating the same procedure, he found a small window that slid open when he pushed on it. At least five feet above the ground, he used the built-in shelving underneath it to scramble up the side of the building and tumbled inside. After groping around for a light switch, he was surprised to find himself in a bathroom right out of a western movie.

The sudden whoosh of propane heated air being pushed through the ducting woke me. *Six o'clock already?* One peak at the nearby digital clock confirmed my suspicions. About to throw back my warm covers, I realized it was Saturday and my day off. Delighted, I pulled them closer and turned on my side. Drifting back into the land of slumber, I became aware of heavy breathing in my ear. "Not now, Bubbles. Go lay down."

The breathing morphed into licking. "Ugh, stop that," I said, using the edge of my sheet to wipe off the dog slobber. "Can't you wait a little longer?" A pathetic whine indicated the urgency of the situation, so I gave in and got up. Pausing just long enough to add a pair of sweats to my oversized Green Bay Packer T-shirt, I shuffled to the backdoor and pulled it open. "Okay Dog, go do your thing," I said, leaning against the doorjamb. The Shorkie took one step, dropped his haunches, and looked up at me. "Now what?" Bubbles barked but didn't budge from his spot on the doormat.

"Just go outside," I said, encouraging the small dog with my foot. That's when I realized it had snowed—a lot. "No wonder you didn't want to go out there. You'd disappear. Hang on a sec." I stomped into my rubber boots, grabbed the snow shovel from its permanent place on the small back porch, and shoveled the six steps that dropped into the backyard. Figuring at least one load of laundry was in my near future, I shoveled a path to the small pump house that doubled as a laundry room. Then I shoveled an area on the lawn for the dog to use.

"Come on," I called to Bubbles when I was finished. The dog looked at me. "This is all you get." He stood and finally trotted down the steps and over to where I was waiting. "And no pooping in the path," I added as I headed back inside.

Carrying the snow shovel through the house, I went out the front door and cleared those steps and the sidewalk from the house to the driveway. Looking forward to spending the rest of the day in front of the fireplace, I figured it was as good a time as any to feed the horses. As I trudged toward the barn, grateful my boots were taller than the top of the snow, I marveled at the peaceful beauty surrounding me, each tiny snowflake sparkling like microscopic diamonds in the bright sunshine.

"Good morning boys," I called to the two geldings sporting their shaggy winter coats. Raven, a black thoroughbred I'd purchased for endurance competitions while living on the east coast, trotted back and forth, tossing his massive head. Mac, on the other hand, just stood nearby, patiently waiting for his serving of hay.

Captured during a wild horse roundup several years ago, the smaller, dark brown mustang had been adopted and saddle broke by one of the wranglers. Eventually, he'd traded it to a fellow wrangler who ended up being arrested during a kidnapping investigation. Certain circumstances left Mac without a place to stay, so I'd offered to stable him until the wrangler could come back to get him. That was two months ago, and while I really hadn't planned on owning two horses, he was a real sweetheart and a nice companion for Raven.

Under normal circumstances, I'd feed Raven in his stall, but because it was too small to accommodate both animals, I threw several flakes of hay into the lean-to shelter on the east side of the barn for them to munch on. Glad I'd drained and rolled up the hose the last time I'd used it, I was able to fill the antique bathtub that served as the water trough. By the time I'd done all that and headed back to the house, I was chilled to the bone.

Back inside, I pulled off my boots, slid my feet into my fuzzy slippers, and pulled on my plush robe. Then I put on a pot of coffee to help warm me on the inside.

A scratch on the backdoor reminded me I'd left Bubbles outside. I swung the door open and was greeted by a shivering dust mop sitting on the stoop. "Sorry, Dog. Come on in." Ignoring me, he trotted through the kitchen, his toenails clicking on the linoleum floor, and into the living room where he curled up in his favorite spot next to the heating vent.

"Good idea," I said, pouring myself a large cup of coffee. Moving into the living room, I wrapped up in one of my snuggle blankets, turned on the television and started surfing for the perfect movie to watch. I'd just selected the 1933 version of *Little Women* starring Katharine Hepburn when, as if from far away, muffled notes began to play. "Where's that music coming from?" I asked my canine companion. A lack of response indicated I was still being ignored. A second verse and I suddenly realized it was my new smartphone. I dashed into my bedroom and checked the charger on the nightstand. Nothing. Bent at the waist, I began tossing articles of clothing that had been strewn across the bedroom floor until I picked up the jeans I'd worn last night. Louder music and a vibrating front pocket signaled the location of the missing phone.

Curious who could be calling me so early on a Saturday, I was less than pleased when I saw it was the Modoc County Sheriff's Dispatch. I tapped the green dot. "Hello?"

"Hey, Sarah. It's Ira."

"Hey, Ira. What's up?"

"Got a lady concerned about a missing person. I offered to send another deputy over to take the report, but she insisted on speaking with you."

"Fine." He gave me the number, and I disconnected without saying goodbye. Hoping for a quick solution, I dialed the number.

It rang once and then a female voice said, "Hello?"

"Hi. This is Deputy Murdock."

"Oh Hon, I'm so glad you called."

"Sal?"

"That's right. I need your help. Henry is missing!"

"What do you mean he's missing?" I returned to my spot on the couch, feeling this conversation could take a while.

"He was supposed to come to breakfast and he never showed up."

I glanced at the clock hangin on the wall. "It's just barely eight o'clock."

"But he said he'd be here at six. That was two hours ago."

"Well, we got at least a foot of snow here last night."

"That's more than we got in Cedarville."

"Maybe he's just running late," I offered.

"Could be I suppose, but it's so unlike him."

"Have you tried calling him?"

Sal laughed. "Oh, Henry doesn't have a cell phone. Says the last thing he needs is a way for someone to be pestering him all the time. I'm just so worried. Would you mind going up to the mine and checking on him?"

I grimaced. Last thing I wanted to do was go tromping around in the snow. "Where exactly is he supposed to be?"

"The Moonlight Mine. It's just off Highgrade Road on the way to Dismal Swamp."

Oh great! "Look Sal, I'm not sure I even have a way to get up there."

"What if he's stranded? Oh my poor, poor Henry," she wailed.

"Calm down Sal," I said, holding the phone away from my ear. "Let me make some phone calls and see what I can do. Is this your cell number?"

She sniffed. "Yes."

"Okay. Call or text me if you hear from him or he shows up."

"Of course. And thank you. Thank you so much."

We disconnected, and I sat staring at the television, no longer interested in the antics of the March girls. I had no idea who to call or how far away this Moonlight Mine was. I went to find it on the large map of Modoc County I had on the wall of the sunroom which doubled as my office. Wishing I had a magnifying glass, I finally found it and calculated the distance to be about ten miles. Too far to ride Raven, who might have actually enjoyed a romp in the snow, I figured the only way the county-issued Ford Explorer or my own Ford Dooley could possibly make the trip was if I had chains for all the tires, which I did not. I considered Remy's Land Cruiser but rejected it for the same reason as my own rigs. But then I remembered his four-wheeler. *Maybe it's light enough to ride on top of the snow.* And if so, I needed to be dressed as warmly as possible.

Leaving the couch once more, I refilled my coffee, wandered into my bedroom, and began digging through my dresser. In no time at all, I located my synthetic long-sleeve shirt and leggings as well as my ear warmer headband, which I tossed onto the unmade bed. Plowing through my closet, I came up with my fleece pullover and Sorel boots but couldn't find either my insulated ski pants or the matching jacket. "They have to be here somewhere," I said to the small dog who had joined me mid-search. "Maybe I hung them in the other room."

Bubbles followed me into the back bedroom, hopped up onto the hide-a-bed sofa and lay down in his favorite spot when watching me work out with my Tae Kwon Do sparring dummy. I swung the closet door open, but before I could begin my search, something caught my eye. "Hey, I'd forgotten all about these," I said, picking up a miniature red wardrobe trunk dotted with small black paw prints, and matching round case. I held them out for Bubbles to see. "Remember these?"

As soon as the small dog saw what I had, he sprang to his feet, baring his teeth and snarling. "Okay, okay. Take it easy," I said, returning them to the floor of the closet. Couldn't say I blamed the little tyke.

When he belonged to my sister, she'd dress him up in fancy feminine doggie clothes, including shoes on his feet—all four of them—and carry him around in a huge handbag. But when she sent Bubbles to stay with me while she traveled to Europe for work, he'd chewed his way into the trunk and shredded everything inside except for one tiny cowboy boot. The other case contained portable dog dishes trimmed with sparkly rhinestones, but Bubba— as Remy likes to call him—prefers the empty whipped topping bowls I've set out for him. Needless to say, the day Alexis came to get her dog, he growled at her and has been with me ever since.

Resuming my search, I finally found the insulated clothing I was looking for. Ten minutes later, I had on my cold-weather gear, as well as my Smith and Wesson .38 Special in its shoulder holster, and was ready to hike over to Remy's. "Come on, Bubbles. Want to go on an adventure?" He approached the front door I was holding open, took a long look outside, and returned to his spot by the heating vent.

"Yeah, that's where I'd rather be myself." Then I closed the door and headed for my neighbor's. Tramping through the snow reminded me of the ski trips I'd made with Sue James, a good friend and former colleague from the Federal Bureau of Investigation. I hadn't seen her for almost a year. *Maybe it's time for another ski trip.*

A few minutes later, I was surprised to see Remy straddling the very four-wheeler I was hoping to borrow and plowing his driveway. He was dressed in his usual plaid shirt, work pants and boots but had traded his black felt cowboy hat for a buffalo plaid wool hat with fleece-lined ear flaps, which kind of reminded me of Elmer Fudd. Even more comical was the small, white goat standing on the seat behind him. Her name was Millie and, after mistaking her for a missing alpaca, I'd rescued her from a large sagebrush in the middle of nowhere. Questioning my ability to take care of the animal, Remy had promptly adopted it and named her after his tiny, white-haired granny.

"Morning Sarah," he called when he spotted me. He made one last pass before shutting down the engine. "I see you're out enjoying this wonderful snow we got."

"Morning, Remy. Actually, I'd rather still be in my pajamas sitting on the couch, but I got a call about a possible missing person."

"Oh, who's that?"

"Remember the guy we met last night at the café?"

"You mean Haywire?"

"Yeah, that's him."

Remy stepped off the ATV and started for the house, the goat right on his heels. "Come on inside, I've got a fresh pot of coffee on. That'll warm you right up."

I followed my neighbor into his double-wide mobile home and sat down in my usual spot at the kitchen table covered with a red and white checkered tablecloth. Millie trotted past me and curled up on the blanket next to Remy's recliner. "Do I smell sausage gravy?" I asked.

Remy laughed. "Sure do. And a fresh batch of them biscuits. Would you like some?" My stomach growled loud enough for him to hear. "I'll take that as a yes. Help yourself to some coffee while you wait." He pulled a white Pyrex casserole dish out of the fridge and a plastic bag full of gigantic biscuits out of the bread box. "One or two?" he asked.

"One will be plenty, thanks."

He tore it in half, smothered it with the creamy white gravy and popped it into the microwave. "Now tell me about this missing person," he said as we waited for my breakfast to heat up.

"Well, apparently he was supposed to be at the Wagon Wheel Café early this morning, and when he didn't show up, Sal called the Sheriff's Office."

The microwave dinged, and I explained my phone call with the waitress in between bites. "So I was wondering if you think your four-wheeler will make it up to the mine, and if so, can I borrow it?"

"I think I have something that would be a might better." Remy took my empty plate and set it in the sink. "Finish up your coffee, and let's mosey on out to the garage."

Entering the main section of the long building next to the woodshed, I followed my neighbor to the far left corner and watched as he pulled back a dusty blue tarp, revealing an old, green John Deere snowmobile. "Ain't she a beaut? Breaks trail like a team of huskies pulling a dogsled, but her narrow track and the set of her skis can make her a might squirrelly." He undid the latches and lifted the hood. "I tuned it up and filled up the tank this fall. Never know when I might wanna go for a ride, especially up past your house. Mighty nice country up that way." He turned the key and gave the pull cord a tug. Nothing. He tried again. Still nothing. "Maybe a little starter fluid will help," he said, lifting one side of the bench seat and reaching inside. He pulled out a spray can and squirted a little into what I assumed was the carburetor. After replacing the can in the seat, he tugged on the pull cord again and the snowmobile fired right up. "Still sounds as sweet as the day I bought her," he yelled over the engine noise. After dropping the hood back into place and securing it, he straddled the seat and drove the machine out into the driveway. He stepped off but left it running. "You ever ride one of these?"

I shook my head. "Growing up in the central valley, there wasn't much opportunity to play in the snow."

"Well, there's not much to it. This here is your accelerator," he said, pointing to a lever on the right handlebar. "You work it with your thumb, and these are the brakes. Just like on my ATV over there."

"Got it."

"Go ahead. Take it for a spin."

I straddled the seat, placing my feet like I'd seen Remy do, and gave it some gas. The machine responded immediately, and I rode it down the driveway toward the road, but when I turned the handlebars to the left, centrifugal force caused it to tip too far to the right, and it dumped me off.

Remy hurried over and helped me get it back on its skis. "I told you it was a little squirrelly. Your center of gravity is higher than you'd think, so you gotta really lean into the turns. Give it another try."

I got back on and started for the garage. This time I tried to make more of a sweeping turn to the left, but the damn thing still tipped over.

"Keep your weight more forward when you lean," Remy called, "and lean further."

Again, I straddled the snowmobile and navigated back toward my neighbor. Starting the turn, I stretched out over the front until I was practically resting on the windshield, really leaned into the turn, and the machine tipped too far to the left this time and again dumped me onto my back in the snow.

"You know," Remy began as he stepped over to where I was still supine in the snow, "I've heard tell of folks with no knack for riding a snowmobile, but I wouldn't have believed it 'til today." He righted the snowmobile and shut it off.

"Thanks Remy," I said, rolling over to my knees and getting to my feet.

"And seeings how you're having such a hard time with this, I guess the only solution is for me to drive you up to that there mine."

"I'm sure I can manage. There aren't that many sharp turns in that road, so I should be fine."

"Well, you never know what you'll find up there. You might need backup."

And there it is! I mentally rolled my eyes but had to admit it might be smart to have someone else tag along. I'd patrolled that area a few times since starting my new career as deputy sheriff, and I knew that there were many spots where cell service was not available. "Yeah, that might be a good idea."

"Well then, just give me a few minutes to close up things and get a few more clothes on, and then we can go." He closed the garage door and headed for the mobile home. "Back in a jiffy," he called over his shoulder. A few minutes later, he reappeared still wearing his buffalo plaid hat and dressed in some kind of dark blue coveralls and winter boots. "Good thing this snowsuit still fits," he said as he stuffed the white plastic bag he was carrying into the compartment under the bench seat. "Brought along a few snacks in case we get hungry." He swung his leg over the seat. "Climb aboard." I got on behind my geriatric driver and lightly placed my arms around his waist. "Better hold on tighter than that or you'll be laying in the snow again." He fired up the engine and as he squeezed the accelerator, I scrambled to stay on, tightening my grip and wondering what I'd gotten myself into—again.

CHAPTER 3

B arely pausing at the stop sign long enough to check for traffic, we turned left without tipping over and began the gradual climb up Highgrade Road. The compact, green snowmobile pushed itself through the snow, just like Remy said it would. I guessed our speed at about ten miles per hour and, at that rate, figured we'd reach the mine in a little over an hour.

Snow covered nearly all the sagebrush, leaving only the tops of the tallest ones peeking out, and juniper trees decorated with clumps of snow resembled Christmas trees. As the road curved to the right and traveled along the east side of the ridge we were climbing, I looked across the northern end of Surprise Valley toward Lake Annie, the blanket of white dotted with fenceposts and an occasional ranch house.

Twenty minutes into our ride, the trees transitioned from the squatty junipers to the more majestic pines. We veered left, leaving the valley behind, and traveled for a while through an area so thick the snow ladened trees gave the illusion of driving through a tunnel. Eventually, we came out of the trees onto the western slope of the ridge. The snow was deeper and to the left, the Warner Range, under its layer of fresh snow, looked cold and dangerous. We continued to climb until we came to an intersection, and Remy let off the accelerator.

"I'm gonna shut 'er down for a spell and let it cool off," he shouted loud enough to be heard over the sound of the motor.

"Are you sure that's a good idea?" I hollered back. "What if it doesn't start?"

He killed the engine. "Don't you worry none. She'll start," he said, stepping off. "Gonna stretch my legs a bit." He began walking back down the trail we'd just made.

Deciding that was a good idea, I hiked up the hill instead to check out a sign I'd spotted. Intended for traffic coming the other way, I had to walk past it and turn around. Fort Bidwell was one of the destinations listed and was six miles back the way we had come.

"Looks like we're over halfway there," I told Remy when I got back to the snowmobile.

"Then we should be there in no time." He turned the key back on and gave the pull cord a tug. The engine fired right up. "See there," he said, a big grin showing through his white beard covered with ice crystals. "Told ya there was nothing to worry about."

We climbed on board and continued on our way. Just past the turnoff for the Mount Vida Vista, the road took us back into a more heavily wooded area. Not long after, we emerged into what I suspected was an old burn, and we again could see the eastern slope of the Warner Range. In less than half a mile, the road narrowed again and took us back into the trees. Thicker right along the road, they helped keep some of the snow from piling up, and the snowmobile picked up speed as we climbed higher and higher. Disguised by its blanket of white, the landscape seemed unfamiliar until we reached a steep hairpin turn to the right. Then I knew exactly where I was.

Stopping halfway through the turn, Remy looked at me over his left shoulder and asked, "Which way?" Buried under the snow, the road to the left looked much more accessible than it actually was.

"Stay to the right," I replied, leaning closer to his ear so he could hear me.

"You sure?"

"Absolutely. First time I patrolled up this way, I took that road. It's just a detour that reconnects with this road further up."

"Alrighty then," he said, and we continued our journey. Minutes later, we passed a sign telling us a right turn ahead would take us to Dismal Swamp. I recalled that Sal had told me the mine was on that road. When we reached the intersection, I tapped Remy on the shoulder and pointed to the left. "See, this is where that detour comes out, and we want to go that way," I said, pointing in the other direction.

He nodded, made the turn, and within minutes, I spotted some buildings among the trees off to the right. I tapped Remy's shoulder again and pointed in the general direction. In less than 100 feet, we found the road in and a red sign that read, "KEEP OUT."

"Well, that's not encouraging," Remy said as we puttered past. "Are you sure this here is the right spot?"

"According to the sign on that building over there, this is the Moonlight Mine."

Remy followed the road and stopped in an open area between what seemed to be the cabin Haywire had mentioned and a rickety outhouse.

"Nothing," I said as I climbed off. "No tracks and no vehicle. Not a single sign that anyone's been here at all. I knew this would end up being a wild goose chase after a meandering miner."

"He might've come up here and left before it snowed. How 'bout we have a look-see just to make sure?" Remy suggested.

"I suppose we could, since we're already here. Let's see if we can find a way in." I headed for the back of the rundown building. "Well, that's strange."

"What's that?" Remy asked, coming around the corner, a few steps behind me.

"The door is open."

"Maybe the storm blew it open," he offered.

"Maybe." Snow had drifted against and over the threshold. Cautiously, I approached the entrance. "Don't think the wind did this, though."

"Why do you say that?" Remy peered over my shoulder. "What in tarnation happened here? You think someone broke in and trashed the place?"

The main room of the cabin was in shambles. Food and other supplies were scattered across the floor; the cardboard boxes that had held them were crushed. Scuff and swipe marks could be seen on the dusty floor. The small table was on its side, and one of the wooden chairs had been reduced to kindling.

"Don't think it was a break-in," I said, pointing to an open lock dangling from a hasp attached to the doorframe. "I'm guessing this was some kind of fight." I unzipped my jacket and pulled my phone out of the pocket of my fleece pullover. "This may be nothing, but I want to get some pictures just in case."

Kicking off as much snow from my boots as possible, I stepped up into the cabin and began taking photographs. Remy followed me inside and wandered into an adjacent room.

"Doesn't look like anything there was disturbed," he said when he returned. "Just a suitcase and black garbage sack setting on the..." He stopped and leaned forward slightly. "Hey, wouldja look at that. Is that blood?"

I snapped the last photo and moved over to where

Remy was standing. "Right there," he said, "next to the box of saltines."

"Could be," I said after kneeling down and inspecting the reddish brown spots in the dust. "But not enough to have been fatal." I got to my feet and looked out the door. "And any evidence of what really happened is buried under all this snow."

"What about searching the other buildings?"

"Pointless. Obviously, whoever was here last night is long gone." I tucked my phone back into the pocket of my pullover and zipped up my jacket. "Time to head back."

Halfway to the snowmobile, Remy stopped. He pulled off his Elmer Fudd hat and scratched his head through the short gray hair. "Something just don't set right," he said, pulling his hat back on. "You telling me that two fellas who are going at it, are just gonna stop and drive off together. Ain't never gonna happen. One of 'em either had to hike outta here or is still around."

"Then why didn't they come out when we got here? They obviously weren't staying in the cabin because it looks like the door's been open all night, and there's no tracks indicating someone exited the cabin after the storm." I looked around. "There's no tracks anywhere."

Remy leaned in and whispered, "Dead men don't leave tracks."

"You mean to tell me you think there's a body here somewhere?"

"Well, something had to happen to Haywire, or he'd of showed up for breakfast."

Good grief! "Fine. We'll take a brief look around, and then we're heading back."

"Sounds good to me," Remy said, starting toward a small shed tucked back among the trees at least thirty yards from the cabin. I followed his trail as he navigated around trees and other obstacles hidden under the snow. A quick peak inside revealed a rusted old metal bed springs and a partially collapsed back wall but no body or any other evidence that someone had been there.

"Can we go now?" I asked.

"Just one more place to check, and we'll be on our way." He retraced his steps part of the way back but then veered off to the right.

"The outhouse? You honestly think someone hid in there all night and is still in there?"

"You can't never tell what some folks might do," he countered. "It'll just take a sec." He slowly approached the small wooden building, which listed to the rear so much that anyone seated inside would be in a reclining position, and peered through a crack along the misaligned door.

"See anything?" I asked, my arms folded across my chest.

"Too dark." He stepped back and began kicking the snow away from the door, so he could open it.

I moved in to help—not because I wanted to look inside but because I wanted him to be satisfied that no one was there, and we could go home. With most of the snow out of the way, he tugged on the door. The bottom was still frozen shut and wouldn't budge, but the crack widened toward the top of the door and he peered inside again.

"Sarah," he whispered, letting go of the door and moving back. "There's somebody in there, and I think he's dead."

"Sure there is." Shaking my head, I stepped past him, pulled on the door and looked inside. Henry "Haywire" Heuson sat in the corner farthest from the opening with his head tipped back and his mouth agape. Frost crystals clung to his bushy eyebrows and scraggly beard, and I couldn't tell whether or not he was breathing. "Help me get this door open!"

Remy grabbed hold of the door and together we managed to yank it open. He crowded in behind me as I placed one foot on the raised wooden floor and reached out to check for a pulse. Just as I was about to touch the side of his neck, Haywire's head jerked up, and he raised his right hand, which was clutching a very large revolver.

"Gun!" I threw myself backward and, as Remy and I landed on our backs in the snow, heard the heart-stopping click of a hammer dry firing on an empty chamber. I scrambled for cover, dragging Remy along with me just as the miner exploded from the outhouse.

CHAPTER 4

"Stay here," I told Remy. Then I leapt to my feet and ran after the man as he stumbled toward the cabin, pulling my .38 Special out of its shoulder holster on the way. As I neared the open door, I heard him banging around inside and entered just in time to see him pull a blanket out of the garbage bag on the bed, drag it over to the remaining chair and wrap up in it before sitting down. Then he grabbed a pint bottle that had been sitting on the uprighted table and took a huge gulp of the amber liquor.

I scanned for the handgun but couldn't see it anywhere in close proximity to the man. "Haywire?" I said, holstering my weapon as I moved closer.

"What the hell is wrong with you!" Remy demanded as he stormed into the cabin. "You pert near killed us!"

"Not now, Remy." Without taking my eyes off Haywire, I held out my arm to stop my angry neighbor as you would an errant child.

"N-n-never h-h-happen," the man said through chattering teeth.

"What's that?" I asked.

"N-n-no more b-b-bullets. Gun w-w-was empty." He shivered involuntarily. "Wh-h-ho are y-y-you anyw-w-way?"

"We met you last night at the café," I reminded him. "Sal sent me to look for you."

"F-f-figures." He continued to shiver and took another swig from the pint bottle. "S-s-sorry about the g-g-gun. It was j-j-just a ref-f-flex."

"A reflex?"

"Remy," I said, turning to face him. "Can't you see this man is freezing? How about you build us a fire, and I'll see if I can find out exactly what happened here."

He grumbled something I couldn't quite make out while he gathered up one of the crushed boxes and pieces of the smashed chair. After laying them in the squatty, cast iron stove, he turned to Haywire and said, "Got any paper or matches?"

"P-p-paper should be on a sh-sh-shelf in the s-s-storeroom. M-m-matches were in one of these b-b-boxes."

"Firewood?" Remy asked as he crossed the room to find some paper.

"S-s-still in the t-t-truck. Hadn't unloaded it y-y-yet."

"So where is your truck?" I asked.

"The asshole that attacked me s-s-stole it."

A wad of newspaper in hand, Remy scooped up the box of matches he'd spotted and, in less than a minute, had a fire blazing.

"Let's move you closer, so you can get warm. Then you can start from the beginning," I suggested, helping Haywire to his feet. As he turned toward the stove, the blanket fell off his left shoulder, revealing a bloodstain on his less than spotless T-shirt surrounding a piece of thick metal sticking out of his chest just below his collarbone. Its shape and size reminded me of the Little Debbie Mini Frosted Donuts frequently devoured by fellow deputy and longtime friend, Scott Jenkins. "You said the man attacked you?" I asked, repositioning his chair closer to the stove and carefully putting the blanket back into place as I gently guided him to his seat.

"That's right. I fought back, though. Even got a shot off with my Colt .45 after he punched me, but the coward run off before I could finish the job."

"Henry..."

The man looked up at me. "Most folks call me Haywire."

"Okay then, Haywire..." I glanced at Remy. "I'm thinking that maybe the man who attacked you did a little more than punch you."

"How's that?" he said.

Remy moved in closer, his curiosity in overdrive.

"I'm going to show you something, but I don't want you to panic."

"Haven't lived this long getting my knickers in a twist every time there's a problem," Haywire boasted. "Get on with it."

"Okay." I gently peeled back the blanket covering his left shoulder.

"Hell's bells!" Remy exclaimed as he leaned in. "What in tarnation is that?"

"What are you two gaping at?" Haywire tucked his chin and tilted his head slightly. "Now how'd that get in there?"

"Well, I think..."

"And is that..." He swallowed. "Is that blood on my..." His eyes rolled back in his head as he slowly began leaning to one side. Making a grab for him, we managed to keep him from toppling out of his chair.

Oh great, not another one!

"What is that sticking in him?" Remy whispered as we replaced the blanket around Haywire's shoulders.

I shrugged. "Beats me. My concern is how deep that thing goes."

Haywire moaned and his eyelids fluttered. "What happened?"

"You fainted," I told him, "when you saw the...well..."

"Oh yeah," he muttered.

"Do you know what that is?" I asked, nodding toward his wound.

"It's a hand forged spike they used to string wire in the mine."

"And about how long is the spike?"

"I don't know. Four or five inches maybe. Just yank it outta there," he said, reaching for it with his right hand.

I grabbed his wrist. "Bad idea. You might cause more damage pulling it out." Gently, I moved his hand away.

Remy pulled me aside. "We need to get him off this goldarn mountain."

"Agreed, but how? There's only room for two on the John Deere, so either one of us stays behind or we figure out something else."

He scratched the side of his chin through his beard. "Well, I suppose we could tow him on something."

"Okay. You go see what you can scrounge, and I'll do what I can to stabilize that spike so we can transport him," I said.

Remy left the cabin in search of some kind of sled, and I rejoined Haywire, who seemed to be resting comfortably for the moment.

"We're trying to figure out a way to get you out of here," I said, "but first I need to make sure that spike doesn't move around during the trip."

"How you gonna do that?" the miner asked.

"First let's slip off this wool shirt and see what we've got." Carefully, I removed the shirt, one arm at a time. "Now, I think that if I tear this T-shirt into strips we can use it like a bandage to hold the spike in place."

"But this here is one of my best undershirts," Haywire protested.

"Not anymore. It's got a hole in it."

He let out the same nervous laugh I'd heard last night at the café. "Guess it does at that. Go ahead then, do what you need to do."

Trying not to disturb the area around the spike, I tore the shirt into several strips and weaved them in a figure eight pattern around the spike that went over his left shoulder, under the armpit, back over the shoulder, across the back, under the right arm, across the chest and back to the left shoulder. I used the last two strips to secure his left bicep to his chest, completely immobilizing the shoulder.

"Ain't never been hogtied before, but I bet this comes close," Haywire said when I was finished. Last thing, I helped him back into his wool shirt.

"I think I may have found just the ticket," Remy said as he re-entered the cabin. "Came across an old rusty piece of corrugated roofing that's already bent on one end like a toboggan. I just need something to bend one side a little more so she'll tow straight."

"My sledgehammer's in the storeroom, if that'll work," Haywire said.

"Might just do the trick."

"What about a rope or something to attach it to the snowmobile?" I asked.

"Not sure a rope would work so well. That piece of roofing is liable to cut it. We need a chain or cable—something metal."

Haywire got to his feet. "I can put my hands on a hunk of cable."

"Whoa there," I said, stepping in front of him. "Just tell me where it is, and I'll go get it."

The man sighed as he sat back down. "Fine. There's a collapsed shed off the east corner of the cabin, and seems to me that cable was sticking out from the pile of rubble."

"Okay. Remy, you grab the sledgehammer and see what you can do with that roofing, and I'll try to locate the cable."

Like the doorway into the cabin, the wind had created a snow drift against what was left of the shed. Starting where the snow wasn't real deep, I shuffled along the edge, hoping one of my boots might catch on that piece of cable I was looking for, providing it was still where Haywire recalled seeing it. A couple of false alarms, and in snow up to my thighs, my toe slid under something that caught on the instep of my boot. Lifting my foot as high as I could, I grabbed the object and was elated when I pulled a section of rusty cable out of the snow. Holding on with both hands, I backed away and freed a piece of three-quarter inch cable about twelve feet long.

By the time I'd dragged it past the cabin, Remy had turned the snowmobile around and had the sheet of corrugated roofing in place behind it. "Think this'll work?" I asked.

"Should." He examined both ends. "Not sure how we're going to attach it to the chrome bar that runs across the back, though."

"Gonna have to weave the ends into loops." Haywire had left the cabin and was standing behind us.

Placing his hands on his hips, Remy asked, "And how do we do that?"

"It ain't difficult. I can do it if you've got a flat blade screwdriver I can use."

Remy reached into the compartment under the seat and retrieved the requested tool.

Haywire sat on the end of the snowmobile and pulled one of the ends of the cable onto his lap. Dividing the individual strands of the cable into two bundles, he began unraveling it. "Here." He handed the end to me. "Keep this going until you've undone about a foot of the cable. Hand me that other end," he said to Remy, "and I'll get it started for you to unwind."

"Now what?" I asked when I'd finished.

"Give it here and I'll make the loop." Haywire bent one bundle into a loop and attached it to the other one by wrapping the short piece around it a couple of times. Then he wrapped the other bundle around the rest of the loop, reforming the cable as he went along. "Now, hand me that screwdriver," he said when he reached the bottom of the loop. He grabbed hold of the top of the loop with his left hand and held it steady against his leg while he stuck the tool through the bottom of the loop with his other hand and, using it like the handle on a vise, began turning it. The screwdriver passed down through the cable, weaving the two loose ends into it as if by magic. He pulled the tool out and then did the same thing two more times, each time twisting the cable tighter. "There," he said, holding up the completed loop. My neighbor and I looked at each other, and I consciously closed my mouth.

"Well, wouldja look at that," Remy said.

"Now, all you gotta do is take this end and go around the bent part of that roofing and through this here bar, and then I'll hook the two loops together. "The only thing is..." He hesitated.

"What?" I said.

"You'll have to cut it to get it off the snowmobile."

"Not a problem," Remy said. "That I can do. But before we head out, we need something to put on the roofing that will act like a barrier and keep the snow from rolling up onto the sled."

"There's Haywire's blanket."

"No good. It needs to be something more water resistant."

"Well, I had an old canvas tarp on my load when I got here last night. Threw it off to the side over there." Haywire pointed toward the cabin where an odd-shaped mound was covered with snow. I walked over and gave it a slight kick, displacing most of the snow and revealing an army green tarp that looked like it had been around since the Korean War. I dragged it over and, with Remy's help, folded it to fit on the piece of roofing.

"I think if we pull it up into the bent section," he said, tugging it into position, "and then run the cable around it, that'll help hold it in place." We did as he suggested, passed the end through the bar at the back of the snowmobile, and handed it to Haywire. He again worked his magic and when he was finished, the two loops were hooked together and the make-shift toboggan was secured to the snowmobile.

"We about ready to leave?" Remy asked, looking overhead. "The clouds are rolling in again."

"Soon as we get Haywire settled on the sled, we can go. Do you have a coat?" I asked him.

"In the truck."

"Oh, well then, do you have any other kind of clothing we can add to what you already have on. It'll be a cold ride back."

"I may have a thing or two in my suitcase, and there's at least one more blanket in the garbage bag."

We followed him back into the cabin, and while he looked for warmer clothes, I stacked the food that had been scattered in the attack on the table, and Remy closed down the damper on the stove.

"This about all I can find," Haywire said. He held up a stained sweatshirt with frayed cuffs, a pair of wool socks, and a stocking cap.

"Didn't you say there was another blanket in there as well?" I asked.

"Oh, yeah. Forgot to grab that."

"I'll fetch it," Remy said.

I helped pull the sweatshirt over Haywire's head and get the stocking cap on. I picked up the wool socks. "You need help getting your boots off?"

The miner grinned at me. "Them are for my hands."

"What do you want to do with this?" Remy came out of the small bedroom, a blanket draped over his arm and the Colt .45 in his hand.

"Oh, I can take that," Haywire offered.

"Let's put it in the seat compartment on the snowmobile," I said. "That way it won't get lost if we go over a bump or something. Just make sure it's unloaded."

"Told you, it only had one bullet," Haywire said as Remy tossed the blanket at me and went outside. "And I shot that one at the guy who attacked me." He looked around. "Sure could use something to eat."

"Well, there's all kinds of canned goods we could open. Where's your can opener?"

"On my key ring..."

"In your truck?"

Haywire nodded.

"I see crackers and a box of Nilla Wafers."

"Well..."

"Forgot all about these," Remy said as he re-entered the cabin, holding out a plastic grocery bag. "They're a might cold but there may be enough heat in that stove to take the chill off." He set the bag on the table and pulled out the biscuits he'd made that morning. "Had a few pieces of bacon leftover from breakfast yesterday, so I stuffed them inside. Not gourmet but it should hold us 'til we get back." He placed them on the flat surface of the stove. "Got some water in here, too." He handed each of us a bottle, and we all stood in front of the stove, watching the biscuits.

Unable to wait any longer, Haywire snatched up his and devoured it in seconds. "Ahhh." He smacked his lips. "That sure hit the spot." Then he drained his bottle of water. "Okay, time to hit the road." He started for the door, stopped, and returned to the table. "May need this in the near future," he said, picking up the pint of whiskey I'd seen him drink out of earlier. He slipped it into the hip pocket of his baggy pants and left.

Remy and I ate our own biscuits, and while he grabbed the two blankets and went out to help Haywire get secured on the sled, I closed the door behind us and fastened the lock. After a brief discussion of the best way to ride, we convinced him lying down would keep him out of the wind better and therefore warmer.

As we started toward the road, the temperature had definitely dropped and an occasional snowflake fluttered to the ground. I sat sideways on the seat for the first few minutes or so, making sure that the sled was gliding over the terrain like it was supposed to and not filling up with snow. I also wanted to be absolutely certain that the cable would hold. Everything was going smoothly, so I began to relax. But by the time we reached the hairpin turn, we were riding through heavy snowfall.

"We ain't outta the woods yet," Remy yelled over his shoulder. I had to admit, the man had a way with words.

CHAPTER 5

The young man sat on the bench outside the store in the full sunshine, hoping to stay warm. The sweet rolls he'd eaten for breakfast were long gone. Ravenous, he tore the wrapper off the ready-made sandwich he'd just bought and gobble down the first half in three gigantic bites. Washing it down with half of his soda, he listened to the conversation between two old guys standing off to the side.

"Now that there's snow on the ground, don't know if just having a light bulb hanging in the pump house is going to be enough heat."

"I had trouble with that last winter because the darn bulb burned out," the shorter man said, "so I got one of those small electric heaters with a thermostat and runs on one twenty. I check it twice a week on Sundays and Thursdays just before supper, and it's working great."

"Might need to look into getting one of those," the other man said. "I better get a move on. The missus sent me to get butter for her baking." As he headed for the entrance, the shorter man climbed into the cab of a flatbed pickup truck.

Wishing he could put his hands on a heater, the young man watched the truck travel south. To his surprise, it turned right and pulled into a driveway just past the outskirts of town. Perhaps a walk that direction would be just what he needed.

Traveling through the heavily wooded area was no problem. In fact, we made good progress since we were going downhill and following the trail we had created on the way to the mine. Conditions worsened, however, when we came out in the old burn. Not as sheltered, the wind-driven snow completely obscured the Warner Mountain Range and reduced visibility to only a few yards. Drifting snow had filled in our trail in several places.

By the time we reached the turnoff for the Mount Vida Vista, snow had collected in every crevice on us and the snowmobile. Glancing back at Haywire, I discovered he was completely buried under a layer of snow. "Hold up," I shouted, tapping Remy on the shoulder. "I need to check on our passenger." I stumbled back to the sled through the deep snow. "Haywire, you doing okay?" I asked.

"Tolerable," was the muffled response. "What'd we stop for?"

"Just dusting off the snow," I said as I gave his blanket a good shake, "and checking on you."

"I'm still kicking. Just get me the hell out of here."

"On our way." I trudged backed to Remy and climbed on behind him. "All good. Let's go."

We finally seemed to get ahead of the storm about halfway back to Fort Bidwell, and I knew we were in the clear when we passed a grader plowing the road just before dropping back into Surprise Valley.

Remy pulled into his driveway and pulled the snowmobile over to his early model Toyota Land Cruiser. "Take my rig and get Haywire to the hospital in Cedarville," he said as soon as he shut down the snowmobile's engine.

"You mean the convalescent hospital?"

He nodded. "Entrance for the regular hospital is around back. Just follow the signs for the ambulance."

We climbed off, and he headed for his mobile home

while I helped Haywire to his feet. I had just settled him into the passenger seat when Remy reappeared.

"Here are the keys. I'll lock in the front hubs and then you can throw it into four-wheel drive."

"Thanks, Remy." I climbed in and fired it up. I rolled down my window when he approached.

"Drive careful. I'll go plow your driveway and fetch Bubba."

"I appreciate it. And thanks for all your help. See you soon." I backed up and started down his driveway. When I reached the road, I moved the lever to four high and we headed south.

"How are you doing now?" I asked Haywire as we left Fort Bidwell.

"My shoulder's aching some. Probably feel a lot better without this thing sticking in me."

"I'm sure it would, but we'll let the doctor make that decision. At least they plowed the road so we'll make good time getting you there." I cranked up the heater. "Let me know if you get too hot."

"Don't see how that's possible. Still feel like I'm freezing."

"Hypothermia. It'll pass."

"Sure hope so." He pulled his blankets tighter, leaned his head back, and was snoring by the time we passed the turn to Fandango Pass. We'd just reached the first road into Lake City when my passenger jarred himself awake with a very loud snore. He sat up and rubbed his eyes with his free hand.

"Think I'm finally starting to—hey, stop! That's my damn truck!" He pointed at an older model Dodge, rust over light blue, that had apparently slid off the road and was sitting at a 45 degree angle in the ditch. The plow had completely buried the driver's side when it went by.

I slowed down and we both craned our necks to get

a good look at it. "I didn't see anyone inside. Did you?" I asked.

Haywire had twisted around and was staring out the back window. "Nope," he said when he finally turned around. "That asshole better have left my keys in it."

"I know someone to call that can help get your truck out of the ditch. Oh, phone call." I fished my phone out of my pocket. "Hey, Siri. Redial my last incoming phone call."

"Dialing," Siri replied.

I touched the dot for audio, selected speaker and propped the phone on the small shelf above the dash.

"Did you find him?" Sal asked the second she answered.

"Yes. We're heading for Cedarville right now."

"Thank goodness. Tell him to come on over. He can stay here."

"Well, there's a problem with his truck and...well... there's a problem with him, too."

"Is he hurt?"

"Yes, but nothing too serious." *I hope.* "Can you meet us at the hospital?"

"The hospital!? You said it wasn't serious."

"Oy," Haywire groaned.

"Just meet us there, and I'll explain."

"I'm going there as soon as I get someone to cover my shift," she said and hung up.

"Women," he muttered. Then he looked at me. "No offense."

"None taken."

By the time we passed the airport, the interior of Remy's Land Cruiser had to be well above 80 degrees. I turned off the heater, unzipped my jacket and wiggled out of it. Five minutes later, I veered to the left and drove to the back of the Surprise Valley Hospital. After pulling into the parking spot closest to the entrance, I slipped off my holster and stashed it under the driver's seat. Then I helped Haywire out of the rig, and we went inside.

The lobby had seating for four and was decorated with two potted plants. Twin deer head mounts hung on either side of the two large glass windows separating the receptionist from the public. The clock on the back wall showed it was just after three, and a silver call bell sat on the shelf at the base of the windows under a sign that read, "Ring me."

I stepped up and double tapped the small button on top of the bell. No one came. I tapped it again. I was about to tap it a third time when Herb Leibowitz poked his head around the doorframe.

"Why Deputy, what can I do for you?" he asked, stepping into the receptionist's area.

"I have someone that needs to be seen by the doctor," I replied, nodding my head at Haywire.

"Oh well, let me find someone to help you." He stepped through the doorway and turned right.

A few moments later, a very pregnant woman wearing holiday scrubs appeared, her condition giving the snowman on her top a three-dimensional look. "How can we help you today?" she asked.

"I'm Deputy Murdock, and I have a victim of violence that needs to be seen by the doctor."

"Oh, I see." She sat down at the desk and tapped a few keys on the computer. "Name?"

"Henry Heuson," Haywire said.

"Have you been in our facility before?"

"Not that I can remember."

She asked him a few more basic questions and then said, "So what type of injury do you have?"

"Well..." He looked at me. "Help me get this sweatshirt off, wouldja."

I carefully pulled it up and over his head, and then removed the wool shirt.

"I got this spike sticking in me."

The woman's eyes widened. "Be right back," she said as she rushed out. In less than a minute, the side door crashed open, and she ushered out a short, stocky man wearing new tan Carhartt bibs over a red union suit and a matching Carhartt coat. Something about him seemed familiar, but I couldn't quite figure out where I'd seen him before.

"Okay Stan," the woman said. "Doctor says there's nothing in your ears, so the buzzing isn't coming from..." She leaned closer and whispered, "Them."

"Them?" Haywire asked.

The man nodded. "Aliens."

"Aliens?" I looked at the woman. She shrugged her shoulders and smiled.

"Ayup," the man said. "Aliens." Then he walked out the door.

Like a lightning bolt to the brain, I realized Stan was the man I'd seen at the alpaca ranch near Eagleville a few months ago.

"Right this way," the woman said, holding the door open. We followed her across the short hallway and into the exam room. "Sit right here," she told Haywire, patting the end of the exam table, "and I'll get your vitals." As I leaned against the wall, she took his temperature and measured his blood pressure. "The doctor will..."

The door burst open and a woman about my age with curly red hair swept up in a messy bun breezed in. "Hi, I'm Dr. Frances Hood, but you can call me—hey, I recognize you!" she said when she saw me. "Last summer in Alturas. Didn't you bring in a woman with purple feet?" The Santa heads dangling from her ears jangled as she spoke.

"Dr. Franny, right?"

"That's right."

"I didn't expect to see you here."

"Well, I rotate shifts at various hospitals in Modoc County. Keeps it new and exciting." She stepped over to the small sink and began washing her hands. "Especially when *you* bring in someone to see me." She pulled a handful of paper towels from the dispenser and studied Haywire as she dried her hands. "I can honestly say I have never seen anything quite like this." She tossed the spent paper towels in the trash and pulled on a pair of latex gloves. "Are you in a lot of pain?"

"It's aching some but not too bad."

"I don't see any injury in the neck area," Dr. Franny said, gently turning his head from one side to the other. "How's your breathing?" She pulled a stethoscope from the pocket of her white coat and listened to several places on Haywire's chest and back. "Lungs sound normal, but there could be penetration of the chest cavity which could result in tension pneumothorax." She slipped the stethoscope back into her pocket.

"How's that?" Haywire asked.

"Oh sorry, a collapsed lung. Did you notice spitting any blood?" she asked as she palpated his shoulder and down his left arm.

"Nope."

She checked his pulse and then asked, "Can you wiggle your fingers?"

"Yup," he said, moving each finger back and forth.

"Hmm, looks like it missed the subclavian artery." Dr. Franny turned to the nurse. "Emily, I think we need to get a picture of this before we do anything else."

"I'll go call Ray," the nurse said, moving toward the door.

"And..." Dr. Franny continued as she leaned closer to the donut-shaped metal object, "I'm thinking we need to start an IV and get some antibiotics into our patient."

"Uh, Doctor..." The nurse stepped closer. "The emergency IV kit was used last week," she whispered, "and we haven't received its replacement yet."

The doctor sighed. "Ok then, at least get the Rocephin." She turned to Haywire. "Do you know when your last tetanus shot was?"

"Well, let me see. Cut my hand back in '08 on a piece of rusty metal, and I believe that was last time I had one of them tetanus shots."

"Then definitely a tetanus shot," Dr. Franny said to the nurse. "And be sure..." She was interrupted by a continuous clanging of the call bell. "Go. I'll make the call to the x-ray technician." They both left the tiny room.

"Well, looks like we have a few minutes to kill," I said. "How about you tell me about what happened up at that mine last night?"

"Told you. Some guy attacked me and then stole my damn truck."

"Did you know who it was?"

"Don't think so, but it was pretty dark. I didn't get a good look at him."

"Where do you think he came from? Was he hiding out there?"

"Well, here's the deal. Didn't notice anything when I drove in and the lock on the door hadn't been jimmied. I started unloading the truck and had everything but the firewood moved into the cabin when I was jumped. We fought fisticuffs for a while, knocking over the table and busting the lamp. Now it's dark and the next thing I know, he's got me pinned to the ground and punches me." He nodded toward the rounded end of the spike embedded near his left shoulder. "At least I thought he'd punched me. Meanwhile, I'm groping around, and my fingers find my revolver that I'd set on the table, and I swing it across in front of me," Haywire said, demonstrating the motion, his right hand imitating the gun. "The barrel makes contact with something, and I hear the guy groan. I rock to one side to get out from under him and fire off a shot. Then I hightail it out of the cabin and run for the truck to get more bullets. I only carry one in the revolver for emergencies, but before I can put my hands on the box of ammo, I hear him coming after me. I run for the outhouse, figuring I could get the jump on him when he opened the door, but instead he drives off in my truck."

Voices that had been barely audible beyond the closed door escalated. "Look here Hon, I need to see Henry!"

Haywire looked at me. "Sal," we said in unison.

"I better go see what's going on." I opened the door. "Don't go away." After crossing the hallway, I slowly opened the door and peered into the lobby. Sal spotted me right away.

"Sarah!" she exclaimed, moving toward me. "Where's Henry?"

"Ma'am!" The pregnant nurse inside the receptionist area rapped on the window. "I told you, you have to wait here."

I stepped into the lobby. "Actually, Sal's the reason I found him. Would it be all right if she saw him for just a few minutes?"

"Well..." The nurse looked around. "I suppose. But just for a minute."

I showed Sal the way to the exam room.

"Oh Henry," she said when she stepped inside and rushed toward him, but he held her off with his right hand.

"What is it? What's wrong?"

He pointed at the metal spike.

"Omigod! How did that happen?" she asked as she leaned closer.

"Some asshole jumped me up at the mine and stabbed me with this." Haywire gestured at the spike again.

"How serious is it?" Sal asked.

"Not sure yet," I interjected. "Doctor wants to get it x-rayed before deciding what to do."

"My poor Henry. I told you..."

Before Sal could finish, the doctor pushed a wheelchair through the exam room door. "Time for your x-ray. Oh hello," she said when she spotted Sal. "I'm Dr. Franny."

"Sally Smith. I'm a friend of Henry's here."

"Pleased to meet you. Now," she said to Haywire, "let's get you over to imaging."

"Don't need no wheelchair."

Dr. Franny smiled at him. "Hospital policy."

"Don't understand what all the fuss is about," the miner said, sliding off the exam table. "Just pull the damn thing out and be done with it."

"All in good time. But first we need to determine what kind of internal damage has been done."

Haywire plopped down in the wheelchair. "Then let's get this over with." As I watched the doctor wheel him past a large linen closet and into the next room barely ten feet away, I had to agree with Haywire; the wheelchair seemed a bit much.

While Sal and I waited, the nurse came in with a small stainless tray holding two syringes, placed it next to the sink and left. Almost immediately, she returned with Haywire. "It'll just be a few minutes, and then the doctor will be in with the results," she said as she reached out to help him back onto the exam table.

"I ain't no invalid," he said, pushing her away and settling on the end of the table.

"No, of course not." She quickly maneuvered the wheelchair through the door and pulled it closed behind her.

"Now Henry, there was no cause to be rude," Sal said. "She was just trying to help."

"Well, don't need no help. Just want to get this thing removed and get out of here. I'm starving."

"As soon as we're done here, I'll take you to the café and have Cookie fix whatever you'd like before I take you home," Sal said. "Have you got another shirt or something?"

I held out the two articles of clothing I was holding. "Got his wool shirt and a sweatshirt here, but the rest of his stuff is still up at the mine."

"That'll do just fine," Sal said, taking the items from me.

The door swung open and Dr. Franny entered, followed by the nurse. "Good news," she began, "it doesn't look like the spike has entered the chest cavity and there were no visible nicks on any of the bones."

"So then you can pull it out and I can get out of here," Haywire said.

"Well, I'm afraid it isn't that simple. Because it has penetrated so deeply, I believe the best way to remove it is with surgery. Unfortunately, this hospital isn't equipped for surgery, so we will need to transport you over the hill to Alturas."

"Oh for cryin' out loud!" Before anyone could stop him, Haywire reached over with his right hand and yanked out the spike.

We all gasped, and then Dr. Franny started barking orders. "Hand me a pair of scissors and grab some gauze!" The nurse yanked open the top drawer and rummaged through it until she found the requested implement. As soon as she handed it over, she pulled open the cupboard above the sink and grabbed a box of gauze pads. In the meantime, Dr. Franny began cutting away the T-shirt I'd torn into strips and used to stabilize Haywire's injury.

"Here, Doctor," the nurse said as she clawed at the top of the box, trying to get it open. With one last tug, the flap came loose and gauze pads flew everywhere.

"We will need to irrigate this," the doctor said, frantically gathering gauze pads and applying them to the wound.

"Right away, Doctor." The nurse turned back to the cupboard and began pulling out supplies.

"Be careful when you remove the gauze," I began, "and don't let him see it because..."

But it was too late. Dr. Franny had already pulled the first handful away from Haywire's wound, and although there wasn't much blood, as soon as he saw it, his eyes rolled back and he collapsed onto the exam table.

"...he can't handle the sight of blood."

"Henry!" Sal exclaimed, moving closer.

"Let's step outside," I suggested, taking her by the arm and ushering her toward the door, "and let them take care of him."

Taking advantage of his unconscious state, the doctor rolled him on his side and, with the nurse's help, began irrigating the wound. We squeezed by them and stood in the hallway, listening to the hushed voices of the two women as they continued to treat Haywire's wound. Finally, we heard him speak, and Sal visibly relaxed. I was about to excuse myself when Dr. Franny stepped out and joined us.

"I think he's going to be fine, but that is quite a deep, penetrating wound. I'll give him instructions on what to do and what to watch for, but he will need to have it looked at in a week or so."

"Yes, Doctor," Sal said. "I'll make sure he follows your directions. Be sure of that."

"Well, now that he's in good hands..." An explosive yell followed by a string of expletives interrupted me.

"What's going on?" Sal asked.

Dr. Franny smiled. "Sounds like the nurse just gave Henry the shot of Rocephin. Very painful."

"Let him know I'll call when I can arrange to get his truck pulled out of the ditch," I said to Sal. "Otherwise, I leave him in your capable hands." Glancing at the clock on my way out, I figured I'd be back home just about dark. *So much for spending a snowy day by the fire!*

CHAPTER 6

"**B**ubbles, cut it out!" I said, yanking the sheet over my head to evade the sandpapery tongue of the canine that insisted on sharing my pillow. "Give me a few more minutes." I burrowed further down into my warm bed, but before I could drift off to sleep again, Bubbles began whining and frantically pawing at the covers.

"Okay, okay." I threw them back and chased the tiny mutt to the backdoor. While he did his business, I dumped some Folgers into the Mr. Coffee and returned to my bedroom for sweats and slippers before starting a new fire in the fireplace. That done and not wanting to venture out into the cold once I'd settled in, I stomped into my boots and trudged down to the barn to feed the horses.

The cloudless sky was a deep blue, and the snow sparkled in the bright sunshine. It was much colder than it looked, however, and I wished I'd grabbed a jacket. Back inside, I threw another log on the fire and let the dog in. Then I poured myself a cup of coffee, grabbed my phone, and curled up on the end of the couch where Bubbles was waiting for me.

"Guess I better text Cindy and see when her uncle can help pull Haywire's truck back on the road," I told him. Cindy Evans was the head dispatcher at the Modoc County Sheriff's Office, and her uncle, Bert Evans, drove the tow truck owned by his tire shop.

Hey, Cindy. Got a favor to ask.

It was a few minutes before she replied.

Hi Sarah. Whatcha need?

Can you ask your uncle if he can pull a truck out of a ditch for me?

Sure. Give me a minute or two to see what I can find out.

I turned on the television and surfed the channels while I waited.

Sorry but Uncle Bert says he's swamped. Still working on the list of calls he got yesterday but should be able to come over the hill first thing tomorrow morning.

Sounds good. Give him my cell and ask him to let me know when he heads over the pass so I can meet him at the café and show him where the vehicle is.

Will do. Stay warm.

Thanks. You too!

Next I called Sal and explained the situation. "I'll call when I hear from the tow truck driver," I added. "Can Haywire meet me at the café in the morning?"

"Of course, Hon. Thank you."

We disconnected, and I pulled my snuggle blanket up under my chin. Settling on a *Twilight Zone* marathon, I entered the mindless state of binge watching. That is, until my phone began playing its not yet familiar tune. A muscle between my shoulder blades tensed as I closed one eye and cautiously peeked at the screen. *Pete!* Owner of the Silver Spur Saloon in Cedarville, Pete Yarbrough and I had become good friends, going on adventures and actually coming to each other's rescue a few times as well as other enjoyable activities. I exhaled loudly and accepted the call.

"Hi, Pete."

"Howdy Sarah. Whatcha got going on today?"

"Not a whole lot."

"Great! How would you like to go on a snowmobile ride? A buddy of mine asked to park his trailer and two snowmobiles at my place while he moves and told me I could use them if we ever got snow. Whatd'ya say?"

"Funny you should ask." I quickly summarized my adventure the day before, concluding with, "So I'm sure you'll agree, I've had quite enough fun in the snow for a while. I plan on holding down this couch for most of the day and, if I get inspired, maybe have a soak in the hot tub later."

"No problemo. There'll be plenty of opportunities to ride this winter."

"I'm sure there will be—just not today."

"I hear you. Later." And he hung up.

Debating on whether or not to leave the comfort of my nest and get another cup of coffee, I closed my eyes and lightly dozed until loud banging on the front door jolted me awake.

"Sarah!" A male voiced called followed by more banging. *Now what!* When the voice called my name a second time, I realized it was Pete. *How long have I been asleep?*

"Coming." I scrambled to my feet and hurried toward the door. Flinging it open, I found my friend standing on the top step and hugging two large paper bags. "What are you doing?"

"Trying not to drop these," he said as he pushed past me and strode into the kitchen. I followed and Bubbles, curious to see what was going on, trotted into the room and sat at my feet. "Thought maybe you'd like some company," Pete said after setting the bags on the table.

"Oh you did, did you?" I peered into the bags. "What's all this?"

"Makings for chili and cornbread à la Yarbrough," he said, unpacking some of the ingredients. "And beer, of course. Got a big pot of some kind I can use?"

I flashed on the disastrous meal my sister had attempted to cook during her rather brief visit last spring, and an involuntary shudder traveled up my spine. "Let me see what I can come up with." I moved around the table and stepped into the large pantry behind the fridge. Not highly skilled in the kitchen, proper cooking equipment has never been high on my list of "must haves," but my mother insisted on purchasing a set of pots and pans when I joined the Federal Bureau of Investigation and moved to Virginia. I perused the selection and retrieved one I thought would be suitable. After giving it a good rinse, I set the large pot on the table next to the cans of beans, trays of ground meat, and packets of spices.

"Expecting more people to drop by?" I asked.

Pete chuckled. "Only way I know how to cook it, but it freezes great." He picked up the pot and started to place it on the stove but stopped. "What happened to this?" he asked, showing me a small, precise dent in the side of it about halfway from the top. "Looks like it's been shot."

"Well, isn't that strange," I said, suppressing a grin. It had happened months ago; more of a glancing blow, but the resulting ricochet had murdered a bag of flour. "Coffee?"

"Huh? Oh yeah, please." Pete placed the pot on a large

burner and turned the knob to its highest setting. While I poured him a cup of coffee, he tore the plastic wrap off the meat, which sizzled when he dropped it into the heated pot.

Not wanting to miss any of the entertainment as well as possibly learning something, I retrieved my coffee, turned off the television, and sat at the table. When Pete asked about knives, a cutting board, and other things he needed, I explained where he could find each item. Soon, the chili's aroma began to permeate the kitchen, and Pete, after refusing my help, set about cleaning up the mess.

"Now," he said, placing the last washed item in the dish drainer, "it just needs to simmer for a couple hours. I'll whip up the cornbread just before we eat." He joined me at the table. "So, what do you want to do while we wait?" The twinkle in his crystal-blue eyes was a good indication as to what he had in mind, but I had other plans.

"Be right back," I said as I pushed my chair back. After stomping into my boots again and remembering to grab my jacket, I went out the front door and tromped through the snow toward the bathhouse.

The first thing I did was switch on the small space heater. Next, I sprayed down the rock-lined sides of the custom hot tub, seated the plug, and opened the faucet all the way, so the water coming from the geothermal spring would be as warm as possible. Then I headed back toward the house.

Pete had retrieved his black backpack from his truck, changed into sweats and a long-sleeve thermal shirt, and was reclined on the couch, scratching Bubbles' ears. "Well?" he asked as I passed through the living room on my way to the bedroom.

"It should be ready by the time we get down there. I just need to change."

A few minutes later, I stepped into the bathroom. "Do you need a towel?" I called.

"Yes, please." Having left his spot on the couch, I found Pete in the kitchen, stirring the pot of chili. "This should be just fine until we get back." He looked down at the small mutt sitting nearby. "You ready for a swim, Bubbles?"

"Oh you won't get him to go outside," I said. "I had to shovel a path just for him to go to the bathroom."

"Is that so?" he asked the dog. "Maybe he just needs a better enticement."

"And what might that be?"

"A ride. Isn't that right, Boy?" Bubbles jumped to his feet, tail wagging. "Well come on," Pete said, patting his chest, "let's go." Without warning, the dog launched himself into Pete's arms.

"How on earth did you get him to do that?" I asked.

He shrugged. "Seems I just have a way with animals." Then he grinned at me. "Kinda like stopping a runaway horse."

"Oh shut up and get going," I said, pushing him toward the door.

The small heater had taken the chill off the bathhouse, and the water had almost reached the top of the hot tub. We quickly slipped out of our clothes and into the warm water and were soon joined by the cunning canine. Two of us floated weightlessly, enjoying the invigorating mineral-laden water. The third happily paddled around, occasionally lapping at the water with his tongue.

"Now, this is how I prefer to spend a chilly, winter afternoon," I said.

"Can't argue with that," Pete said as he lay back and closed his eyes.

Two bowls of chili and three beers a piece later, we lay comatose on the couch, watching one of the multitudinous versions of *A Christmas Carol*.

"Gotta favorite?" Pete asked, nodding at the television.

"Well, the older black and white ones are rather quaint, but I don't much care for the one with George C. Scott. I enjoy this one with Patrick Stewart even though the Ghost of Christmas Future is rather lame."

"Spoiler alert."

"Oh, yeah. Sorry. But I think my favorite is the musical with Albert Finney. I love the songs, and Alec Guinness is fabulous as Jacob Marley."

"Uh huh," Pete said as he stared at me.

"What?"

"Very analytical."

I sneered at him. "Well, you asked. Do you have a favorite?"

He nodded. "The one with the Muppets."

"The Muppets?" *Good grief!*

He nodded again. "I'm a huge Gonzo fan."

"Somehow, I'm not surprised."

"Well, what do you want to do now?" Pete asked when the movie was over.

"As much as I have enjoyed the food and especially the company, I have a ton of things to do before I go to bed."

"I could give you a hand," he offered.

"I'm sure you could, but somehow I think you would be more of a distraction."

"And that's not a good thing?"

"Not today. Besides, tomorrow will most likely be a busy day." Little did I know, that was an epoch understatement.

CHAPTER 7

I'd just dropped Bubbles off at Remy's and started south on County Road 1 when my cell phone rang. I pulled the Ford Explorer over in front of the historic town hall in downtown Fort Bidwell and accepted the call.

"Murdock."

"Howdy, Sarah. Bert Evans. Just calling to let you know I'm starting over the pass."

"Perfect timing. I'm heading to Cedarville myself. I'll meet you at the Wagon Wheel Café."

"See you there."

After we hung up, I called Sal and let her know I'd be at the café in approximately thirty minutes. Then I continued south, slowing as I passed Haywire's truck. The berm of snow still blocked the entire left side of the vehicle, and I wondered how difficult pulling it back onto the road was going to be.

I pushed through the door of the café a little past eight and found Haywire sitting at the counter, sipping coffee and chatting with the fellow seated next to him. It was obvious right away that his baggy pants and stained sweatshirt had been through the laundry, and the wool socks he'd worn on his hands when we brought him down off the mountain were visible above the tops of his boots. The only new addition to his ensemble was a blue sling cradling his left arm.

"Good morning, Hon," Sal said as I approached the counter. "Pour you a cup of coffee?"

"Maybe later," I replied. "I'm expecting the tow truck any minute. You ready to go?" I asked Haywire.

"Sure am." He grabbed his stocking cap off the counter and his wool shirt from the back of his seat. That's when I noticed he'd also had a thorough cleaning as well as a close shave. "Let's go."

We headed for the door, and Sal called, "You be careful Henry Heuson."

"Yeah, yeah," he replied, waving her off without turning around.

"How's the shoulder?" I asked as we strolled toward my patrol unit.

"It's a bit stiff but not too bad." He glanced back at the café before slipping his left arm out of the sling. "Sal throws such a hissy fit when she sees me do this," he explained as he put on his wool shirt and pulled the stocking cap down over his ears. "Doc says I'm not to use the arm for at least a week but that's a royal pain in the..." He stopped when a heavy-duty tow truck equipped with a seven-foot plow pulled in next to us.

"Howdy," the driver said after rolling down his window.

"Morning, Bert. Don't believe I've ever seen you in this rig before."

"I use that flatbed you're familiar with when I know I'll be transporting a vehicle. This here is primarily used for pulling out stuck ones and plowing, of course."

"Of course." I smiled. "Hey, I appreciate you coming over the hill this morning."

"Sure, sure. Just glad it could wait until today. It amazes me how many people don't know how to drive in the snow."

"Can't argue with that," Haywire said, slipping his arm back in the sling.

"Bert, this is Henry Heuson and..."

"Most folks call me Haywire."

"Pleased to meet you," Bert said, offering his right hand through the open window.

"And..." I began again, "it's his truck we're pulling out."

"That so?" Bert said.

"Yeah, some son-of-a-bitch stole it and then put it in a ditch."

"Well, at least he didn't get very far with it," Bert offered.

"True enough," Haywire said, nodding his head. "True enough."

"It's between the two roads into Lake City," I said, "on the lefthand side of the road. I'll stop at the top of the hill with my lights on to hold any vehicles heading north. There's good visibility coming from the other direction, and most of the locals will know to just detour around us."

"Sounds like a plan. Let's go see what we can do." Bert rolled up his window and edged toward the road. Haywire and I got into the Explorer and followed him.

Arriving at a good spot to hold traffic, I parked at an angle across the northbound lane and lit up my overheads. Bert had pulled up next to Haywire's truck and was outside his rig looking over the situation. With an obvious plan in mind, he climbed back into the cab of the tow truck and began making several passes with the plow, moving small amounts of snow from the side and rear of the stuck vehicle.

"He's pretty good with that thing," Haywire said.

"I imagine he's had lots of practice."

With most of the snow removed, Bert parked the tow truck behind Haywire's and facing in the opposite direction. Then he got out, grabbed a shovel and began digging out the rest of the snow blocking the driver's side door.

"Time to get to work," Haywire said, bailing out and heading down the short hill. Not sure what he had in mind, I shut down the engine and followed him. We reached Bert just as he moved to the back of the truck and began digging out the rear axle.

"Looks like we're about ready to heave this on outta here," Haywire said.

"Soon as I get the winch hooked up, we'll be good to go."

"Great." He stepped over and yanked the door open.

""Whoa!" Bert exclaimed. "Hold on now. What are you doing?"

"Checking on my keys," he said, struggling to hold the door open. When he shoved his back into it and pulled his arm out of the sling again, I moved in to help. "Thanks." He stepped into the cab, bracing his feet against the transmission hump. "I'll throw 'er in neutral while I'm in here. Can be a bit temperamental."

Bert looked at me, and my shoulders gave a slight involuntary shrug. "Fine," he said, "I'll drag the winch cable over."

While he did that, Haywire balanced on one leg and mashed the clutch to the floor with the other. Then he grasped the gearshift with his right hand and gave it a good tug. Nothing moved. He let off the clutch a little and tried again, but the gearshift remained where it was. "Come on, you damn thing," he grumbled. He continued pedaling the clutch until finally, the transmission popped into neutral.

"We ready to go?" Bert called from the back of his tow truck, having secured the cable to Haywire's truck.

"Yeah, I think so," I hollered back.

"Get him outta there, and I'll start the winch."

"Come on Haywire, time to climb out."

"Nah, I'm good. May need to steer." He quickly pulled the door out of my hand, and it slammed shut.

"He refuses to get out," I called to Bert, who mumbled something I couldn't quite make out.

"Then stand back," he warned. "I don't have all day." He pressed a button and the winch began to whine.

As I stood on the other side of the road and watched the rust over light blue Dodge creep backwards out of the ditch, a light snow began to fall, and I zipped up my winter duty jacket.

"Make sure he puts the brake on," Bert hollered when the truck was back on the road. He reversed the winch, giving the cable some slack.

"You got the emergency brake on?" I asked when Haywire opened the door.

"Sure do." He grinned at me. "And she's back in gear, too."

By the time Bert had disconnected the cable and Haywire had checked out his truck, looking for any damage, the snowfall had gotten heavier and was sticking to everything.

"Time to dig out my coat," Haywire said. He walked around to the passenger side of his truck and tugged on the door. A hideous shrieking of the rusty hinges was followed by a loud clank as it swung open. "What the hell is all over my seat? Omigod, is that..." He disappeared from sight.

Bert and I looked at each other and rushed over to where we'd last seen Haywire. He was laying supine on the road. "What the heck happened to him?" Bert asked.

"No idea," I replied. "Help me stand him up before he

gets a chill." We sat the man up and, after a minute or two, got him to his feet. "Here, hold him steady," I said, leaning him against the bed of the truck, "and I'll look for his coat." Peering into the cab, I immediately spotted what had made Haywire pass out. A significant amount of blood had soaked into the saddle blanket seat cover that was so worn out it must have been installed when the truck was new. "I think I know why he passed out," I called to Bert. "He must've seen this bloodstain in here."

"Bloodstain? From what?"

"Long story, but he must've been a better shot than he thought." I snapped a picture of it with my phone before searching for his coat, which I found stuffed behind the seat.

"Here, you feeling better?" I asked as I wrapped it around Haywire's shoulders.

"Yeah, yeah," he said, pushing us off and slipping his arms into the sleeves of the dark grey Filson Mackinaw jacket.

"If there's blood on the seat, how's he gonna drive back to town without passing out again?" Bert asked.

"That's a good question."

Haywire shook his head. "If you grab that old blanket from under the seat and throw it over the back, I'll be just fine." While I did what he asked, he locked in the front hubs. "Okay, all set."

"Not quite," Bert said, holding out the clipboard he'd retrieved from the tow truck. "I need to know whose nickel is going to pay for this."

"Given the circumstances, I can check and see if the county might pay, but..."

"How much?" Haywire asked.

"A hundred and seventy-five bucks, unless you got insurance."

Haywire dug his wallet out of his hip pocket and pulled out a card. "Take Triple A?"

"You bet." Bert recorded the necessary information on his form and had Haywire sign at the bottom. "That will do it," he said, handing back the card. "Thanks."

Haywire put the card back in his wallet and started to climb into his truck. "Oh, almost forgot," he said, sitting on the edge of the bench seat with one foot still on the ground. "When do I get my Colt .45 back?"

"I'll try and drop it by the café in the next couple days."

"Much obliged." Then he got the rest of the way in and drove off, leaving Bert and me standing in the middle of the road.

"Give you a ride back to your rig?" he asked.

"Sure, that'd be great."

"So, wanna fill be me in regarding that bloodstain?" We'd turned around and were heading back up the hill.

"Apparently, Haywire got attacked the night he went up to his mine," I began, "and during the struggle he'd managed to fire off a shot with his handgun. He wasn't sure whether or not he'd hit anything but from the looks of the seat in his truck, he did."

"Gotcha." He pulled up next to my patrol unit. "So, based on what you saw today, there may or may not be a gunshot victim out there, and you're going to give the guy who shot him back his gun?"

"When you put it that way, it does not sound like a smart thing to do but..."

"Unit 113, Modoc County."

I reached up and keyed my mic. "Go ahead Modoc."

"I've got a vehicle off the road on Highway 299 west of Cedarville. RP says it's just south of Cedar Creek Lower Trailhead and might be 11-85, but I haven't tried to contact anyone yet."

"Well, your uncle is sitting right next to me. Want me to ask him if he can respond?"

"Oh hey, Uncle Bert."

I keyed the mic again and nodded at him. "Hello Cindy," he said.

"Well?" I asked. "Got time to check it out with me?"

Bert nodded. "Sure, don't see why not. It's on the way back over the pass."

"Modoc, 113 and tow truck responding."

"Copy, 113. Time 9:47."

I hopped out of the tow truck and climbed back into my patrol unit. With the additional snow on the road, I dropped it into four-wheel drive and pulled in behind Bert.

By the time we reached the location, another two to three inches of fresh snow had fallen. The vehicle we were looking for had slid off the road backwards and gone into a small ditch. The front bumper and grill of an older Ford of some kind was all I could see poking through the lower branches of the trees on either side of it. The rest of the vehicle was so completely hidden by the surrounding vegetation, I couldn't even tell what color it was.

"Modoc, 113. We're 10-97."

"Copy, 113. 10-97."

Although we'd both parked as far off the road as possible, our rigs still blocked most of the westbound lane. I hoped the visibility would hold and oncoming traffic see our flashing lights and not complicate the situation. As I approached the vehicle, the limbs of one of the trees began to move even though there was no wind, and an individual, who I assumed was the driver, emerged. Dressed in jeans, Sorel boots, a Carhartt coat and black stocking cap, I was fairly sure it was a young boy. But when I looked at the freckled face with its blue-green eyes and shock of red hair poking out from under his hat, I was certain. "Billy Henrickson, what are you doing up here?"

He shoved his hands into his jeans pockets and motioned toward the vehicle in the ditch.

"Yours?" I asked.

He nodded.

"Shouldn't you be in school?"

"It was late start today, so I went up to check on the ski area."

As someone who enjoyed downhill skiing, I clearly understood his excitement at the first good snow of the season. "Oh, so then this happened..."

"On the way down," he broke in. "I even had it in four-wheel drive and everything."

"So what's the story?" Bert asked, finally joining us after seeing to necessary preparations on his tow truck.

"Bert, this is Billy Henrickson. Billy, Bert Evans."

"Henrickson...you Hank's boy?"

"Yes, Sir."

"Well, you've grown some since the last time I saw you. So how did you manage to do this?" he asked, nodding at the Ford.

"On the way down," Billy began, "I thought I was going too fast, so I stepped on the brake. That caused my truck to fishtail into the guardrail. I must've hit it hard enough to spin me, and I ended up there."

"You were lucky you didn't connect with one of these trees. Let's see if we can get you outta here," Bert said. Using the shovel he'd been holding, it didn't take long for him to expose the front axle. Once that was done, he tromped around the truck, checking it out. "This is going to be a bit tricky," he said. "Because of how the truck is sitting between these two trees, I'm going to have to pull him straight out, which means I'll be blocking the entire road." He looked back toward Cedarville. "There's plenty of time to see what's going on from this way, and having to stop suddenly while driving uphill isn't nearly as dangerous as when driving downhill."

"Agreed," I said. "I'll head further up the hill and park somewhere so people can see me and have plenty of time to stop. Call me when you're clear."

"Will do."

"Good luck," I said as I started back toward the Explorer. After navigating around the tow truck, I drove as far as the lower trailhead and turned around. The snow continued to fall as I headed back down. Reaching the bottom of the straightaway, I pulled over as far as I could and, for the second time that day, lit up my overhead lights. Watching in my rear view mirror, it wasn't long until I spotted a car approaching. I held my breath as I watched its rear wheels slide first one way and then another. Finally, it stopped a short distance behind me, and I let out a huge sigh of relief. Hoping the current storm would keep traffic to a minimum, I got out to inform the driver of the situation and that it shouldn't take too long. Then I climbed back into my patrol unit and cranked up the heat.

Muffled music and a vibrating sensation woke me a short while later. I quickly dug out my phone and hit the green dot. "Murdock."

"Hey Sarah, we're all clear down here."

"Did you have any trouble?"

"Nah, popped right outta the ditch. He's got a little damage on the rear passenger panel from smacking the guardrail. Other than that, he was good to go, so I sent him on his way."

"That's great. I don't suppose he had one of those magic insurance cards like Haywire did."

Bert chuckled. "I didn't have the heart to charge him.

It was kinda on my way back, and he's got enough grief having to explain to his father what happened."

"That's really nice of you, Bert. Thanks again for all your help."

"You bet. And speaking of on my way back, I'm gonna get going before this snow gets any deeper over the pass."

"Don't blame you at all. Bye." I disconnected and dropped my rig into low. Turning off the overhead lights, I glanced in the rear view mirror; two additional vehicles had pulled up behind me. Waving at Bert as we passed, I remembered to radio dispatch. "Modoc, 113. I'm 10-98."

"Copy 113, 10-98."

I took it easy coming down off the hill and when I'd reached the center of Cedarville, my stomach let me know it was time for an early lunch. However, Cindy had other plans for me.

CHAPTER 8

Pulling up in front of the Wagon Wheel Café, my radio went off. "Unit 113, Modoc."

"Go ahead, Modoc."

"Got a call about a 594 and...maybe...a possible 187 but..." A long pause. "Negative on an 11-44."

Wait, what? How can there be a homicide with no body? "Ten-nine?"

"RP says someone broke in and made such a mess of the place that it looks like someone got murdered, but there's no body."

"Copy. What's the 20?"

"Winje's Farm on County Road 1. Hang on, and I'll pull up the address."

"No need," I said. "I know right where that is."

"RP, first of Jeanette, will be waiting for you in front of her shop, right off the driveway."

"Copy that, on my way." Ignoring my stomach's protest, I backed out and headed north. The additional four inches of fresh snow on the road slowed me down considerably. When I finally arrived, I was rather surprised to see a familiar Toyota Land Cruiser parked in the driveway, and an even more familiar elderly gentleman in his Elmer Fudd hat standing next to a woman with cropped white hair. I got out and retrieved the camera from my evidence case in the back of the Explorer.

"About time you got here, Partner," Remy called as I approached the two of them.

"Hello, Remy. What are you doing here?"

"Heard your call on the scanner, and I thought you'd need some backup." Looking rather pleased with himself he added, "Besides, you know we've been talking about checking this place out, remember?"

And the truth comes out. "Yes, I remember," I said, smiling at the woman, "but this may not be the best time to do that." I extended my right hand. "Deputy Murdock, ma'am. And you are?"

"Jeanette Winje. My husband and I own this place," she said, tugging her coat more tightly around her. The long white sweater she wore over a dark brown turtle neck and matching pants reminded me of the ones I'd seen at the Mountain Weavers.

"I see. You called about a break-in?"

"Yes. We got home late last night after being gone for a week, and when my husband went to plow the back driveway this morning, he spotted footprints coming from our cottage and a set of tire tracks nearby. He came and got me, and together, we went to check out the cottage. That's when we saw the blood."

"Blood?" Remy asked. If he'd been a dog, I'm sure his ears would've perked up.

"Remy..." I began.

He raised both hands in surrender. "I know, I know. Let you handle it."

Turning back to Jeanette I asked, "Did you go inside?"

"Well, yes. But as soon as we realized someone had been in there, we left and called 911."

"And where is your husband now?"

"He drove up to Bidwell to get a few things at the store to tide us over until we can get over the pass and do some shopping in Alturas."

"I see. Well, let's go take a look."

She led the way along a shoveled path to a small white building I assumed was the cottage she was talking about. The front door was tucked back under a covered porch, and a deck which was connected to it, ran halfway down the left side of the building. To the right of the door, the building extended about twelve feet, as if that section had been added on at a later date.

"You can see where the footprints come off the front steps and go off in that direction," she said, pointing to what now looked more like indentations rather than footprints, the falling snow having almost completely filled them in. "My husband had just started clearing the driveway when he noticed the tracks. He shut down the tractor so as not to disturb them." She turned and indicated a small window on the front of the addition. "Whoever it was must have climbed in here."

"And why do you think this is how they got in?" I asked.

"Well, that window's lock is broken, and we saw this." She pointed to a dark smear just below the ledge.

I leaned in closer. "Yeah, that could be blood."

"Wait 'til you see inside." Jeanette stepped onto the small porch and opened the front door.

The cottage was essentially a one-room cabin that had been divided into different sections. The living room was directly ahead, complete with a chair and matching footstool, a television perched on top of a bookshelf, a small gas fireplace and a sofa that helped separate it from a kitchen area to the right. A small dinette set was just to the left of the front door, and the back portion of the room had been designated as the bedroom area. Under normal circumstances, the place must have looked quaint; however, at the moment it was more like a scene out of a low budget horror movie.

Blood droplets dotted the white flooring, and there were blood smears on the light switch and most of the kitchen cabinets. The bed had definitely been slept in and there were a few bloodstains on the bedding.

"The worst of it is in here," Jeanette said, leading the way to the right and stopping in the doorway of a small, rustic-looking bathroom.

"What in tarnation happened in there?" Remy exclaimed, peering around me.

The white sheer curtains, splotched with blood, hung from a rod that had been knocked askew. Blood that had dripped onto the floor had been tracked through, leaving partial shoe prints on the black and white checkered flooring. The white painted cupboards under the counter had been smeared with blood during an obvious ransacking, and the sink was full of bloody towels.

"Your guess is as good as mine," I replied. Trying not to disturb anything, I began taking pictures. "Is that your first aid kit?" I asked, nodding at the open plastic box and its contents scattered across the counter.

"I think so," Jeanette said. "We keep one in here for emergencies."

"Looks like they used some butterfly bandages, a couple gauze pads and some adhesive tape." I took a couple more pictures and then moved back into the main room. "Although there seems to be blood everywhere, I don't think anyone was killed here. More like someone was injured and tried to clean themselves up."

"Well, I guess that's somewhat reassuring, but who would do this?" she asked, looking around.

I had my suspicions, but they weren't going to get me anywhere in the investigation, especially if that person had left the area as I suspected. "I have pictures of the partial shoe prints, and I can see if there are any viable fingerprints in any of these smudges of blood, but unless this individual is in the system, the chances of finding out their identity are very slim."

"Please do whatever you can, so I can get started on cleaning up this mess."

"Yes, ma'am. I'll go get my evidence case and…"

"Let me get that for you, Partner," Remy said and hurried out the door.

"Is he really your partner?" Jeanette asked.

"Well, more like a self-appointed one, but he has actually been helpful from time to time." I pulled my notebook out of my hip pocket. "If you don't mind, jot down your name and contact information for me. That way if I find out anything in regards to who may have done this, I can let you know."

"Certainly," she said, taking the notebook as well as the pen I offered.

While she did that, I removed my jacket and laid it across the back of the sofa after making sure it wasn't going to come in contact with any evidence. Then I checked out each blood smear, looking for any kind of partial or complete fingerprint. I located a pretty good one on the inside of a kitchen cabinet door and another one on the lid of the plastic first aid kit.

"Here you go," Remy said a few minutes later, setting my evidence case on the small dining table.

I opened it and removed a pair of gloves, two hinge lifters to collect the fingerprints, a roll of photo scale stickers and a Sharpie.

"You know," Remy said, "as I was getting this here case, I was wondering if maybe you shouldn't get a sample of the blood for DNA in case you end up with a suspect."

"Oh, I think that's a very good idea," Jeanette agreed.

"I can do that, but again with nothing to compare

it to…" I gave a little involuntary shrug. To the pile of supplies, I added a packet of sterile swabs, a swab box and a disposable vial of distilled water. "Okay, all set." I pulled on the gloves and, using the Sharpie, wrote the date and location on the swab box as well as the backs of the two print lifters. Then I tore open the package holding the twin swabs and twisted the cap off the vial of distilled water. Moving into the bathroom where there were larger smears of blood to choose from, I moistened the swabs with a few drops of the water and rubbed each one back and forth across the sample in order to get as much blood as possible. "I'll need to let these dry," I said laying them across the swab box so that the tips weren't touching anything. Then I grabbed the roll of scale stickers, placed one below each of the two prints I'd located and took pictures; first with my digital camera and then with my phone, so I could email them to Josh Green, the lab tech at the Sheriff's Office. That done, I exposed the adhesive strip on one of the hinge lifts and placed it over the bloody fingerprint I'd found on the cupboard and applied pressure. Peeling it off, I was pleased to see that the entire print had been preserved. I repeated the same procedure on the first aid kit. Last thing, I dropped the swabs into the swab box, placed all the evidence I'd collected into a small Manila envelope, and secured it inside my evidence case.

"That should do it," I said, gathering up the trash and folding it into the used gloves as I peeled them off. I placed them in my case along with my camera.

"Oh, these are yours," Jeanette said, handing back my notebook and pen.

"Thanks." I slid them back into my pocket and put my jacket on. "Like I said, we may or may not get anything from what I've got here." I picked up my evidence case. "But I'll be sure and let you know if we do."

"I appreciate that," Jeanette said, opening the door.

"It was mighty nice to meet you," Remy said, reaching his right hand up as if to tip his black felt hat—that is, if he'd been wearing it.

"Come on, Remy. Time to go," I said, ushering him out the door and down the steps.

"Thank you and good-bye," Jeanette called and closed the door.

"Sure don't envy the cleanup they've got in there," I said, following Remy along the path back to the vehicles.

"Well, hell's bells! In all that excitement, we forgot to ask about looking in that there shop," Remy said when we reached the main driveway.

"Probably not the best time anyway." I put my evidence case into the back of the Explorer. "Well, I should get back on the road." My stomach let out a loud growl. *And straight to lunch.*

"Yeah, I oughta get home myself and see what the two holy terrors have been up to."

"Hopefully not too much. See you after work." I climbed into my patrol unit. "Modoc, 113."

"Go ahead, 113."

"I'm 10-98. Definite on the vandalism but negative on the 187."

"Oh, thank goodness...uh, I mean, Copy 113. Time 13:21."

I fired up the engine, waved to Remy as I backed out of the driveway and headed south.

It was after three when I exited the Wagon Wheel Café, and the heavy snow had continued to fall. I started the Explorer and called Josh while it warmed up.

"Go ahead and email me those fingerprints, and I'll forward them to the DOJ and see if we get a hit," he said after I'd explained what evidence I'd collected. "The blood samples will need to be sent off to a lab."

"With the weather the way it is, I'd rather not drive over the pass this afternoon unless I have to."

"No worries, just refrigerate them, and they should be fine."

That shouldn't be a problem today! "Will do, and I'll send those prints to you as soon as I hang up."

"Sounds good. Bye." He disconnected, and I immediately called Cindy. A self-proclaimed "Apple Girl," she'd shown me the basics of operating my new iPhone. I could send and receive calls and texts, open and read my emails and even reply if necessary. But as far as emailing a picture, I was clueless.

"Hey Sarah," she said when she answered. "What's up?"

"I need some help emailing Josh some pictures on my phone."

"Sure thing, on one condition."

"Okay. What's that?"

"You fill me in on what went down at Winje's Farm."

"Deal. Now, how do I do this?"

"Go to your photos and select one you want to send. When it opens, there's a square with an arrow coming out of the top along the bottom of the screen. Press that, then you can select more pics if you have more than one to send."

"Okay, hang on a sec." I pulled my notebook out and jotted down what Cindy had said. "Got it, then what?"

"Press the mail icon at the bottom and a new message will pop up. Type in Josh's name and his email should appear. Select it, type something on the subject line, and then hit the up arrow at the top of the screen."

"Up arrow at the top," I muttered as I finished writing down her instructions. "Got it."

"Anything else I can help you with?" Cindy asked.

"No, that should do it. Thanks."

"Welcome." She hung up.

A few minutes later, I'd managed to email the two pictures of the fingerprints and was headed to Rabbit Traxx to fuel up. The attendant was pushing snow with a quad equipped with a plow similar to Remy's when I pulled in. I parked next to the pumps and got out.

He dismounted and headed over when he spotted me. "Afternoon Deputy," he called as he approached.

"Hey Mike," I replied. "Looks like you're fighting a losing battle."

"That's for sure." He lifted the nozzle of the nearest pump and began filling the tank. "Can't seem to get ahead of what's falling from the sky."

I had to agree; it was hard to tell the plowed areas from the unplowed ones. "Aren't you cold?" I asked. Every inch of his hooded sweatshirt was drenched. "You're soaked."

"Yeah," he said, looking down at himself "I seemed to have misplaced my new coat somewhere. Pretty sure I had it down here Saturday but can't for the life of me locate it. It's a dandy, too—what they call a puffer jacket, dark grey with a waterproof outer layer and an adjustable fur-lined hood."

"Sounds like just what you need on a day like today."

"My wife bought it for that very reason. That's why I can't bring myself to tell her I've misplaced it."

"Well, I hope you find it." I moved to the back of the Explorer and opened the cargo door. After removing a large Ziploc bag from my evidence case, I filled it with snow from one of the berms Mike had piled up and put it back in the case. Then I laid the envelope containing the blood samples on top of it and closed it up. *That ought to keep them cold enough until I get home.*

I paid for my gas, wished Mike good luck on his plowing, and headed back out on patrol. A couple hours later, I was on the way home. It had finally stopped snowing, and I was looking forward to a bowl of the chili Pete had left behind.

CHAPTER 9

"Where the hell are you?" his uncle demanded. "Your mother says you're not answering your phone and haven't been home in almost a week."

"Phone's been turned off. And besides, you told me not to come back without the money. I'm still trying to get it," he said.

"Where's that?"

"The sign on the post office says Cedarville, California—wherever that is."

"How did you get there?"

"Hitched a ride, but got more than I bargained for."

"So what's the holdup?"

"It's complicated—but I'm working on it."

"Well, quit screwing around and get your butt back here. I need that cash!"

"Chill, Uncle Benny. I told you I'm working on it. I gotta go; my battery's getting low, and I'm not sure how I'm gonna charge it yet." He disconnected, turned off his cellphone, and shoved it into the hip pocket of his jeans.

As I trudged back to the house after feeding the boys their morning flakes of hay, I spotted Remy plowing his way down my driveway. Several inches of fresh snow had fallen overnight, possibly making my journey over Cedar Pass dicey. I considered waiting for him but the bitter cold temperature, for which I was not properly dressed, convinced me otherwise, so I waved at him instead and went back inside.

After a hot shower and my usual strawberry Pop-Tarts and coffee for breakfast, I got dressed, tossed the Manila envelope with the blood samples and fingerprints into a small ice chest along with one of my cold packs, and was ready to start my day.

"Come on Bubbles," I called to the small canine dozing in his favorite spot next to the heating vent. "Time to go." He raised his head and looked at me but didn't move. "Now, Dog." I opened the door just in time to watch Remy clear off the last step.

"Morning," he said, leaning on the snow shovel. "Looks like we got ourselves another dose of this here white stuff."

"Sure does," I said. "And thanks for clearing my driveway and shoveling. You don't really have to do that, you know."

"That's what partners are for."

"Speaking of partners, where's your co-pilot?" I asked, referring to the small white goat that usually rode behind him.

"Way too cold for her this morning."

"I believe Bubbles would agree," I said, glancing at the small dog sitting on the threshold. "Had to practically toss him out the door this morning to do his business."

"Can't say as I blame him. Packing your lunch these days?" he asked, nodding at the ice chest I was holding.

I held it out in front of me. "Taking the blood samples I collected yesterday to the lab guy." I pulled the door closed, forcing Bubbles to join me on the porch as I did so.

"Trip over the pass could be a might tricky."

"Agreed, but I plan on taking my time." I started

down the steps toward my patrol unit. "You want me to follow you to your place and drop off the dog?"

"No need." Remy laid the snow shovel across the four-wheeler's handlebars and climbed aboard. "Come on, Bubba. Time to go." The miniature mutt flew down the stairs and leapt onto my neighbor's lap. "Drive safe and we'll see you this evening," he said before firing up the engine and heading back the way he'd come.

Shaking my head, I slid in behind the wheel of the Explorer and placed the ice chest on the floorboard of the passenger seat. Then I started it up and headed for County Road 1.

Travel was slow on the unplowed road, which was a good thing considering the number of ranchers I had to wait on as they drove their tractors across the main road, clearing snow from driveways and dooryards. Nearly an hour later, I'd just reached the airport when a call came in over the radio.

"Unit 113, Modoc."

I grabbed my mic off the dash and pushed on the button with my thumb. "Go ahead, Modoc. This is 113."

"Got a call about a 484 on Wallace Street in Cedarville. RP, first of Gary, says it's the second place on the right."

"Copy, Modoc." A few minutes later, I pulled up in front of a garage that sat right on the edge of the street. The sectional door had been raised, and a rather thin man of average height was standing in the center of what looked like an auto repair shop, his hands tucked into the pockets of a short denim jacket. He approached my patrol unit as I got out.

"Hi, I'm Deputy Murdock. Are you Gary?" I asked.

"That's right," he said, offering a handshake which I accepted. "Gary Tallow. Thanks for coming."

"Sure. You called about a theft of some kind?"

"In here." He led the way back inside the shop and pointed to the left. "It was hanging right here and now it's gone."

I spotted a large hook extending from the wall next to the open door and about seven feet from the floor. "And what exactly was hanging there?" I asked, taking my notebook and pen out of my shirt pocket.

"My brand new LED work light and a 50-foot Dewalt industrial extension cord."

"Can you describe them and were there any distinguishable marks or identifying labels?"

"The light is a neon green and the cord is bright yellow. No labels. Didn't figure I needed to put my name on my own property in my own shop since I wasn't going to be taking it anywhere to get mixed up with anybody else's."

I nodded. "And when were these items taken?" I asked after jotting down the details of what was missing.

"Well, I was real busy all day Saturday. Had three jobs and didn't finish up the last one until about eight o'clock, but I was using the work light for it. I had the door open for a bit Sunday morning while I cleared the driveway and sidewalks with the snowblower, so my wife could go to church."

"And the work light and extension cord were hanging up at that time?"

Gary tipped his head to one side and looked at me for a few seconds. "You know, I didn't notice if they were or not. My wife was yelling at me to hurry up and sweep off her car or she was going to be late, so I just shoved the snowblower back into place over there," he said, pointing to the right, "closed this door, and left through the man door there in the back."

"And yesterday?"

"The shop is closed on Mondays, so I didn't even

come out here. Spent most of the day by the wood stove. But when I came out here this morning to get out the snowblower again, I noticed they were gone."

I finished writing and put the notebook and pen away. "Mind if I look around?"

"Not at all." Gary stepped back out of the way.

"You keep this door locked?" I asked, walking over to the man door.

"Yeah, mostly to keep the neighborhood kids from playing in here."

Close inspection of it and the door jam didn't reveal any marks indicating a forced entry. "And the sectional door? It's kept locked as well?"

"Yes. Turning the latch in here automatically locks it and the only way to open it from the outside is with the key."

I moved outside and looked at both windows, one on each side of the shop, and again found no evidence of forced entry. "Well Gary," I said, leaning against the grill of the Explorer, grateful for the bit of heat coming from the engine, "without any distinguishing marks or labels, it will be very difficult to identify the stolen items. I will file an incident report but at this point that's all I can do."

"That's what I figured," Gary said, "but let me tell you, the replacements will have my name all over them."

"A good idea. Now, if you'll excuse me," I said, pushing off the front of my rig, "I have to get over the pass to Alturas."

"That may take some doing this morning."

That's what I'm afraid of. "Guess I'll find out soon enough." I climbed in and started the engine. After making sure my seatbelt was secure and the defroster set to maximum, I threw it into gear and headed for Highway 299.

Although I had enjoyed skiing with my friend Sue James while living on the east coast, my experience driving in winter conditions was limited mostly to plowed or snow-packed roads. I wasn't too sure what to expect driving in several inches of fresh snow. I was encouraged, however, when I reached the outskirts of Cedarville and spotted tracks coming down off the pass. *At least one vehicle has made it over.* Breaking trail in the westbound lane, I began my ascent.

Travel was slow but steady and with no lateral movements of my patrol unit. I encountered a couple of vehicles heading toward Cedarville before reaching the summit and then a snowplow heading up about halfway down the other side. Pulling onto Highway 395, I was glad to see it had been plowed. The remainder of the trip to Alturas went a little quicker, and I arrived at the office just after ten o'clock.

I pushed through the front door, flanked by large sheets of thick, reinforced glass on either side, and spotted Cindy at her usual spot at the reception desk. On the phone, she waved me on by, indicating she was going to be a while. I lifted the small ice chest in return, headed down the hall to the lab, and set it on the large viewing table in the center of the room. I'd just dumped out the contents of the Manila envelope when Josh walked in.

"Oh hey, Sarah. I wasn't sure I'd see you today what with all the fresh snow."

"Yeah, I wasn't all that excited about driving over the pass myself but figured I needed to get this stuff to you. Here's the blood samples," I said handing over the small cardboard box, "and here are the actual fingerprints I lifted."

He looked at the hinge lifters I'd handed him, pushed his heavy-framed glasses onto his forehead, and looked at them again. "Wow, these really are red. I thought it was just some weird lighting when you took the pictures."

"No, that's blood."

"And where did these come from?" he asked, dropping his glasses back into place.

I quickly explained what I'd seen in the small cottage and what I thought had happened. "Did you get any kind of hit on those prints I emailed?"

"Not a thing. Any idea on who it might have been?"

I shook my head. "I doubt it was a local but may be related somehow to another incident that happened over the weekend."

"That missing person?" Josh asked.

"How did you know about that?"

He laughed. "Ira told me. It was the only call he got Saturday. And you think that whoever went missing did that?"

"No, I found him. I'm thinking that maybe it was the guy he shot."

"Somebody got shot?"

I summarized Haywire's attack, including the firing of the handgun and the bloodstain on the truck seat. "So, the most logical conclusion is that the bullet must have struck the attacker."

"And this...this..."

"Haywire."

"Yeah, Haywire. This Haywire doesn't have any idea who attacked him?"

I shook my head again. "Not a clue. And if you can't tell me," I said, nodding at the prints he was holding, "we'll probably never know."

"Well, I'll get those samples sent off right away," Josh said. "But honestly, if his prints aren't in the system, his DNA most likely isn't either."

"Very true. Besides, I'm betting that guy is probably long gone by now." I closed the lid of the ice chest and picked it up. "See you later, Josh."

"Yeah, see ya."

Cindy hung up the phone just as I came around the corner. "Oh just in time," she said. "Start talking."

"Huh?"

"The supposed murder at Winje's Farm. What the heck happened?"

"Oh, that. Well, looks like someone who was hurt broke in for medical supplies to stop the bleeding and ended up spending the night."

"Must have been lots of blood if the RP thought someone had gotten murdered."

I nodded. "And it was everywhere."

"Ugh, that's gross!"

"I'm pretty sure the grossest part was cleaning it up."

"Oh, for sure."

"So, I was wondering if you'd like..." I stopped when Dirk Sandusky suddenly appeared.

"Here's that report you wanted," he said, handing Cindy the file he was holding.

She smiled at him. "Thank you."

"Murdock, what are you doing here?" he asked as if he hadn't noticed me when he walked up. "Why aren't you out on patrol?"

"I just needed to..."

"And why are you out of uniform?"

I looked down at what I was wearing. "Out of uniform?"

"That's right, out of uniform. Where is your tactical vest you were issued two months ago?"

"Oh, that. It's too bulky to wear under my coat, but it's in my patrol unit in case I need it."

"I see, in case you need it." His voice increased in pitch

and volume. "And just how will you know whether or not you need it?"

It hadn't taken me long to realize what a pompous ass Sandusky was and that he'd had it in for me from the start. I figured it had something to do with my previous employment as an agent for the FBI—I'd heard he applied but failed the psychological evaluation—as well as the fact I'm a woman. Needless to say, every encounter with him seems to turn into some kind of confrontation.

"Come on Sandusky, you know..."

"Undersheriff!" he bellowed, his complexion instantly deepening. "Undersheriff Sandusky!"

"Now Dirk..." Cindy began.

He spun toward her and shouted, "What?"

She took an involuntary step back. "Oh," she said meekly. She and Sandusky had been spending a lot of time together ever since he'd helped me rescue her from a crazed kidnapper. Although I never really could picture them together, she claimed they had so much in common, and that she now understood why he acted like he did.

Things may be about to change.

Seconds ticked by as Sandusky came to the realization of what he had done. "Oh Cindy, I'm..."

She raised her hand, palm out. "Save it. Sarah," she said, looking at me, "thanks for stopping by and filling me in. Drive safely back over the pass." Then she turned to the left, slipped past the end of her counter and disappeared down the hallway.

As quick as I could, I hurried out the front door, leaving Sandusky and his stunned expression alone at the counter.

CHAPTER 10

"Hold your horses," I said as I opened the backdoor. Bubbles circled three times, sat down for two seconds tops, then stood up and circled again, whining the entire time. "Give me a break, Dog. Just go outside."

Another fresh layer of snow about four inches deep had fallen overnight, and Bubbles, in spite of his urgency to pee, was refusing to budge. "You're unbelievable, you know that?" I said, stomping into my rubber boots and grabbing the snow shovel. I quickly cleared the path for the persnickety pooch, threw on a few more items of clothing, and trudged down to the barn.

Returning to the house, I ignored the scratching at the backdoor long enough to pull off my boots and put on a pot of coffee. Then I let Bubbles back in and headed for the shower. Thirty minutes later I walked out the door with an unopened Pop-Tarts package in my teeth, a small dog tucked under my left arm and a sloshing cup of coffee in my right hand.

Remy bustled out his front door when I pulled into the driveway. "Here you go," he said, shoving a foil a packet into my hands when I opened the door. "Figured the plowing could wait long enough for me to whip out a breakfast casserole. There's two big pieces in there to hold you over 'til lunchtime."

I flashed on slabs of the stuff served cold in a livestock

trailer and smiled in anticipation. "Thanks, Remy." I set the packet on the console, tossing the Pop-Tarts package that had been sitting there into the backseat, and scooped up Bubbles. "And this is for you," I said, handing over the dog.

"Come on, Bubba. We'll go have our breakfast and then get to plowing. Have a good day," he said and closed my door.

I chuckled as I backed up and headed down the driveway. However, I only made it as far as the town hall in Fort Bidwell before I succumbed to the sagey aroma coming from the foil packet beside me and had to pull over. I opened one end and removed a three-by-three square of eggy goodness dotted with red bell pepper, chunks of potato, clumps of sausage and topped with melted cheese. I savored the first bite, but it was so delicious I wolfed down the rest. *It's even better when it's hot!* I contemplated eating the second piece but decided to keep it until later, so I closed up the foil packet and set it on the transmission hump right in front of the heater vent in order to keep it warm. Then I began my patrol.

I'd just made it past the sweeping turn to the left, heading due south, when a person on a snowmobile pulled out from behind and passed me. "What the hell!" I exclaimed, reaching for my overheads but stopped when the machine accelerated out of sight. Realizing there would be no high speed chases given the current road conditions, I chuckled to myself and continued on my way. By the time I'd reached Cedarville, I had encountered three more snowmobiles and two quads as well as the tractors I'd come upon yesterday clearing the fresh snow. Acquiescing to the situation at hand, I dug out the remaining piece of breakfast casserole and leisurely continued south toward the county line, waving at everyone traveling by all modes of transportation.

Riding along in the comfort of my heated vehicle rather than clinging onto the back of an ancient snowmobile, I actually enjoyed the beauty of the countryside blanketed in snow, including the forest of tall pines running up the slope of the Warners. And if it held out for another two weeks, it would definitely be a white Christmas.

My return trip brought me back to Cedarville around one o'clock, just in time for lunch. As I pulled up to the front of the Wagon Wheel Café, I noticed Haywire's Power Wagon with chains on all four tires. Going inside, I found him sitting at the counter and looking none too happy.

"What'll you have?" Sal asked when I sat down. She was not her usual bubbly self either.

Although I knew the menu by heart, I always looked at it before ordering, more out of habit than anything I suspected. "Well, I think I'll have...what kind of soup do you have today?"

"Tomato bisque," Sal said.

"Perfect. Give me a grilled cheese and a bowl of soup please."

Sal jotted my order onto her pad. "Something to drink?"

"How about a large coffee-to-go."

More scribbling. "Fries?"

"Not today, thanks. Just the soup and sandwich."

She tore off my order and hung it on the ticket holder hanging over the pass-through window.

"Come on, Sweet Sally," Haywire said when she passed by with the coffee pot.

"Don't call me that!" she snapped. "I told you it's too dangerous." She proceeded to make her rounds, filling cups as she went until the pot was empty. "I'll get you your coffee as soon as I make another pot," she said as she walked by. Within a minute or two, the new pot of coffee was brewing and she was standing in front of Haywire, her hand on her hip. "I don't see what's so damn urgent."

"I need to check on my—I just need to check on my things."

"Besides, there's no telling how much snow is up there, and you are in no shape to go gallivanting around," she said, nodding at the sling on his left arm.

Haywire whipped it off and waved his arm around. "There ain't nothing wrong with me."

Sal folded her arms across her chest.

"Dammit woman, give me my keys!"

She shook her head.

"And just how am I supposed to get back to your place?"

"Same way as I got to work this morning—walk. I'll drive your truck home when my shift is over."

Haywire threw the sling onto the counter in front of Sal and stormed out of the café. She watched him tromped off through the snow for a few seconds before turning her attention back to the coffee maker. She'd just set a large styrofoam cup full of fresh coffee in front of me when Cookie tapped the bell twice and called, "Order up."

"Is uh...everything okay?" I asked when she placed my soup and sandwich on the counter.

"That crazy fool wants to drive back up to the mine. I told him to wait until his shoulder heals and give the snow a chance to melt a bit. But noooo, he's soooo worried about his stuff," she said, making air quotes with her fingers while she said the last word.

"Is he sure he can make it up there?" I asked, dipping a corner of my sandwich in my soup.

"Well, he claims that truck of his is like a tank when it's all chained up and can go anywhere, but he doesn't always think things through." She shook her head as she grabbed the coffee pot and made the rounds again.

I'd just finished my lunch and was adding cream and sugar to my coffee-to-go when my cell phone rang. "Murdock."

"Hey Sarah, it's Pete. I've got a little problem over here at the Spur. You got time to stop by?"

"Sure, I'm just down the street. Be there in a jiffy." *Oh brother, I'm beginning to sound like Remy.* I disconnected and put the lid on my coffee. Then I met Sal at the cash register to settle my bill and headed out the door.

Pete was standing next to his Toyota Tundra when I pulled in. He was wearing his black and white racing jersey with the Rockstar emblem on the front and his riding boots. "I can't believe this is happening," he said as I got out.

"What?"

He ushered me to the rear of his truck where a small trailer was hooked to the hitch. A black Polaris snowmobile with neon yellow trim sat on one side. "It's gone!"

"What's gone? I don't understand."

"Remember I told you that my buddy had left his snowmobiles at my place and that I could ride them if we got snow?"

"Yes."

"Well, what's wrong with this picture?" he asked motioning toward the trailer.

I looked again at the machine. The skis were set a lot wider than Remy's snowmobile and looked like they had independent suspension. The seat was shorter, and the track was larger and more exposed. I was about to tell Pete I still didn't understand when... "Wait, you said snowmobiles. Isn't there supposed to be two of them?"

He nodded. "There were two of them when I parked

here. With the fresh dump of snow, I thought it would be great to take one of them for a run before work, so I towed the trailer over here and took off on this one. But when I got back, the other one was gone!"

"What did it look like?" I asked, taking out my notebook and pen.

"It's a Yamaha. Looks a lot like this one but is red, black and white."

"Got it." I stepped closer to the trailer. "These need a key?"

Pete stared at me for a few seconds. "Yes," he said quietly. He'd had a similar experience with his Harley last summer. Fortunately though, he got it back with only some minor damage. "Did you see anyone riding one of these today?"

"Actually, there were more of these on the road than vehicles this morning."

Pete suddenly got very excited. "Any match the description of the missing one?"

"Well..."

"Oh, come on. As a deputy aren't you supposed to have superhuman powers of observation?"

I glared at him. "Mostly, I was trying to avoid hitting them. They were all over the place, but there may have been one or two with that color scheme."

"Which way were they headed?"

"Only one passed me heading south..."

"You were passed by a snowmobile?"

"Oh shut up," I said, shoving on his shoulder. "I was traveling at a safe speed for the current road condition. And it wasn't the right color anyway. Did you look to see which direction it went?"

"No, I didn't." We walked to the back of the trailer. "Which one of these tracks is yours?"

"This one, going past my truck."

"Then this one must have been left by the thief," I said, pointing to a set of tracks heading toward the back of the bar. We followed them around the building but when we reached the road, a passing snow plow had removed any trace.

"Oh great," Pete said, "that's just great. What am I going to tell Alan?"

"Alan?"

"That's who owns these." He walked back toward the trailer. "So what happens next?"

"I'll fill out an incident report and keep an eye out for it. Probably ought to contact your friend and let him know. His insurance may cover theft. In the meanwhile..." I reached up, removed the key from the remaining snowmobile and handed it to Pete. "You may want to keep this in your pocket."

"Oh you're quite the comedienne, aren't you?" he said, snatching it out of my hand.

I shrugged slightly as I walked back to my patrol unit. "See you later." Heading back the way I had come, I turned left and followed Highway 299 to its end. The location of a recent wild horse roundup, it looked a lot different under a thick layer of snow. After parking, I sat long enough to enjoy my now lukewarm coffee. When it was gone, I drove back to Cedarville, turned right and headed north. Taking County Road 18, I traveled along the western edge of Surprise Valley to Lake City. Instead of driving past Gus Miller's abandoned house, I veered left onto Upper Lake City Road and followed it back to the main road just above the spot where Haywire's truck had slid into the ditch.

It was completely dark by the time I'd picked up Bubbles and pulled down my own driveway. Having fed the horses and started a fire, I had just settled into a corner of the couch with a microwaved bowl of chili when my cell phone rang. Securing my dinner out of the reach of my mischievous mutt, I grabbed it off its charger on my nightstand.

"Hello?"

"It's back."

I didn't recognize the male voice. "Sorry?"

"It's back. The snowmobile is back."

Pete! "It is? What happened?"

"Well, Hank Henrickson was pulling in and saw someone messing around the back of the trailer. He hollered at them when he got out and they took off, so he came in and got me. And there it was, big as life, sitting behind the trailer."

"So you're telling me the thief brought it back. That's a first. Did Hank give you a description?"

"All he could tell was it was some young guy wearing a dark coat with a hood."

"And which direction did he go?"

"Toward the center of town. Anyway, he helped me get it loaded and I'm on the way back to my place to drop the trailer and secure the snowmobiles."

"Don't forget to grab the key," I teased. Silence. "Pete?" The call ended. "Well Bubbles," I began, setting my phone down on the cushion next to me, "I may have taken that a bit too far."

CHAPTER 11

The young man stood in the center of the room, surveying his handiwork. Every bag, box, shelf, and cupboard had been thoroughly searched and the contents scattered but with no results. The money was not there. He kicked the box of saltines, sending the small, white squares all over the room. Time for something more direct, he thought as he headed out the door.

Craving a cheap hot dog with all the fixings for lunch, I pulled into Rabbit Traxx and parked in front.

"Hey Deputy," Mike said as I pushed through the door.

"Hi Mike," I replied. "Looks like you get a break from plowing today."

"Sure does. It'll be nice to stay dry for once."

"Still haven't found your coat, huh?"

"Sure haven't, and the wife is beginning to get suspicious. Don't know how much longer I can put her off," he said, shaking his head. "What can I do for you?"

"I came in for one of your famous hot dogs." I continued around the glass counter toward the self-serve area.

"I'd give 'em a few more minutes. Just put some fresh ones on the rollers."

"That's fine." Burned out on eating Pete's chili, I moved toward the large freezer on the back wall. "I'll grab a couple things for dinner tonight while I wait." After perusing the limited selection, I decided on an Asian rice bowl and a box of pizza rolls.

"One or two?" Mike called as he set out a small, red checkered food tray.

Two! Give me two... "Just one, please." I placed my dinner items on the counter, got myself a large Pepsi out of the soda dispenser and set it on the counter, too.

"Here ya go."

I took the tray with a hot dog nestled inside its bun and piled on all the available condiments except the sliced jalapeños. I grabbed a handful of napkins, added a small bag of barbecue chips that was calling my name and paid Mike. After securing my lunch, I dropped the bag of frozen food into the ice chest I'd left in the Explorer since Tuesday, added a Ziploc full of snow to keep it cold, and headed for the park. Approaching from the north in order to get the full benefit of the sun shining through the windshield, I pulled part way up onto the snow berm outlining the park's perimeter in order to get out of the road as far as possible and cut the engine.

I'd just tucked a double layer of napkins under my chin, hoping to avoid any new ketchup stains on the shirt of my uniform and taken a huge bite of my hot dog when my cell phone rang. "Murdock," I managed to get out around the wad of food in my mouth.

"Someone tried to kill Henry!"

I instantly swallowed, nearly choking myself in the process. "Sal?"

"They sabotaged his truck and tried to kill him!"

"Okay, calm down. Where is he?"

"He managed to make it back to town and is here with me at the café."

"Okay, I'll be right there." Two minutes later, I pulled up next to Haywire's rust over light blue Power Wagon parked in front of the Wagon Wheel Café, having wolfed down the rest of my hot dog on the way. I pushed through the door and immediately spotted him seated at the counter. I glanced around at the lunchtime crowd as I made my way over, finding it strange that almost everyone was looking at me and either grinning or laughing out loud. Focusing on the task at hand, I sat down next to Haywire. "So what's going on?"

He turned toward me and his right eyebrow went up. "Well..."

"I told you," Sal interrupted as she returned to the counter, "someone is trying to..." She stopped when she looked at me, the hint of a smile beginning to form. "Uh, looks like you're all ready for something to eat. Can I get you anything?"

"No thanks, I just had lunch."

"Oh," she chuckled. "That explains the..." She placed her hand on her chest and nodded at me. Then she nodded again and pointed at my chest.

Slightly confused, I looked down and was horrified to find the napkins still tucked into the collar of my shirt. *Unbelievable!* As I snatched them off and wadded them up, I felt the heat of my reddened face creeping upward. "Thanks," I said, barely above a whisper.

"Of course," Sal said. "Now what are we going to do about this attempt on Henry's life?"

"Why don't we start at the beginning," I suggested. "What exactly happened today?"

"Well, I left here early this morning..."

"Snuck out you mean," Sal interjected.

"And headed for the mine," Haywire continued. "I had no problem until about six miles above Bidwell. The plow had only gone that far and there was a berm across the road. It took a couple of tries to bust through it, but I made it. Chained up on all four, that truck of mine is just like..."

"A tank, yes we know."

"Sal, please," I said, "let Haywire tell it."

"Fine," she said, throwing her hands in the air. The bell on the front door tinkled against the glass as new customers entered the café. Sal walked the length of the counter, grabbed a couple of menus and met them at their table.

"Go on," I urged. "Then what happened?"

"I threw it into four low and kept going."

"Did you notice any problems with the brakes at all?"

"Not a one, course I didn't use them much going uphill. When I got to the entrance of the mine, I happened to notice that a snowmobile had been there. I didn't think much about it at first because I'd seen all kinds of tracks crisscrossing the road all the way up. But these tracks went right up to the cabin, and when I got out of the truck, I could see footprints heading toward the door and back again.

"Thinking it was just someone looking around, I was shocked to find the door had been forced open and the cabin ransacked. Not only had my supplies been torn into, but the bed had been turned over, my suitcase and the garbage bag of bedding had been dumped and the contents scattered. Whoever it was even tossed everything out of the storeroom and into a big pile in the main room.

"Quick as I could I gathered up my personal belongings and packed up what supplies I could salvage. As soon as I had all that in the truck, I went back inside for my..." He paused.

"What else did you go back in to get?" I asked.

He glanced at Sal who had rejoined us at the end of the counter.

"Was it the gold out of the mine?" she asked. "Do you think that's what they were looking for?"

"Oh hell, that damn mine petered out years ago."

"Then why do you keep going up there?"

Again he paused. "Well, you know I don't trust banks."

"Yes, but what does that..."

"I've been using the mine as my own personal bank."

Sal just stared at him.

"It's where I stash my cash."

"What cash?" Sal demanded.

Haywire paused a third time. "My winnings," he murmured.

"Your what?"

"Oh for heaven's sake, woman. My winnings. Whenever I hit it big, I bring it here for safe keeping in my strongbox."

"And that was still in the cabin?" I asked.

"Yup. Had it hidden beneath the floorboards under the wood stove. In fact..." He patted his waist and then leaned in. "I've got $20,000 to add to it. Just didn't get a chance to before I was attacked."

"On you right now?" I asked.

"Yup, in my money belt."

"Oh my!" Sal exclaimed, dropping into the seat next to Haywire.

"Who else knows about the money you are carrying?"

"Just the bookie I got it from, but he's back in Vegas."

"Okay, tell me about the trip back."

"Once I made it back to the road, I put it in four high for a couple of reasons. First, I had my own tracks to drive in and second, it was downhill. Everything was fine 'til I got to the sharp turn to the left. As I approached it, I put my foot on the brake a couple times to slow down, but the third time the pedal went right to the floor. I was fishtailing so bad, I barely made the turn. I tried to downshift but was going too fast. The emergency brake didn't seem to be working either. Somehow I made it to the section of the road that had been plowed and used the berms along the sides to slow me down enough I could downshift. I finally got stopped when the truck went up a small hill. Then I crept back to town in second gear."

"But all this doesn't necessarily mean someone is trying to kill you. I mean, isn't it possible that the brake lines were worn out..."

"Here's the deal," Haywire said. "She may not be much to look at, but I keep that truck of mine in excellent running condition. In fact, those brake lines are less than two months old."

"Well then, maybe we should just get them checked out." I suddenly remembered my call on Tuesday. "Tell you what, there's a mechanic over on Wallace Street. His garage sits right on the edge of the road. Why don't we take your truck there and have him take a look?"

"I suppose there ain't no harm in that," Haywire said.

"Most likely this is just a coincidence. If someone, in fact, is looking for your money, I doubt they are trying..."

"Unit 113, Modoc."

I reached up and keyed the mic of my portable radio. "Go ahead Modoc, this is 113."

"I've got another 484. Location is a small building on County Road 1, just south of Locust Street. RP, first of John, is on scene."

"Copy." I stood up. "I've gotta go. Give me about 30 minutes, and I'll meet you over on Wallace Street."

"Will do. That'll give me time to get some things secured," Haywire said.

"Just be careful," I warned. "Until we figure this out, pay attention to your surroundings."

"Might feel safer if I had my Colt back."

With everything else that had been going on, I'd completely forgotten about Haywire's gun. And even though I was hesitant to return it, there was no legal reason, at the moment, for me not to. "I don't have it with me right now but can try and get it to you tomorrow."

"Much obliged."

I left the café and headed south. The small building just past Locust Street was easy to spot, and I pulled in and parked next to a Ford flatbed truck. Almost immediately, the driver's side door opened, and a very short man with a slight build climbed down out of the cab. As he approached my patrol unit, the first thing I noticed was his enormous handlebar mustache, which made him look even smaller up close.

"Well, that didn't take long," he said.

"I was just up the road. Deputy Murdock."

"John Johnson. It's this way." He led the way to the shed and opened the door. Two small electrical boxes hung on the back wall and were connected to a large, horizontal cylinder on the floor. Huge pipes coming out of it, disappeared through the floor. "It was sitting right here," John said.

"Uh, what was sitting right there?"

"A space heater. It was plugged in to that socket right there," he said, pointing to the left side of the small building. "Only had it for a couple of months."

I took out my notebook and pen and jotted down the information. "Can you describe the heater?" I asked.

He looked at me as if I had asked him a stupid question. "It's a space heater. What more do you need to know?"

Moving on, I asked, "When was the last time you saw it?"

"I check on it every Sunday and Thursday just before

supper. This being Thursday, I came to check on it this afternoon as me and the wife have plans this evening."

"I see. And do you keep the door locked?"

Again the look. "It's a pump house. Why would I lock it? There's nothing of value in it."

I started to say something but decided against it. "Well, unless it has something unusual about it or an identifying tag or label, there's a slim chance of recovering it."

"Nothing unusual about it and no tag. So, I'm just out the heater, huh?"

"I'm afraid so." I slipped my notebook and pen back into my shirt pocket. "But if something happens to turn up, I'll let you know."

"Yeah, yeah." John ushered me out of the building, closed the door, and headed back to his truck.

I got into the Explorer and backed out onto the road. *What a weird week this has turned out to be!*

CHAPTER 12

"So his brake lines were actually cut?" Remy asked as he parked in front of the Mountain Weavers.

"They sure were." I'd filled him in on how the rest of my week had gone, finishing with Haywire's adventure coming back from the mine.

"Well don't that beat all. Any idea who done that?"

I grabbed the ball of brown yarn impaled by two knitting needles I'd taken home the week before. "I'm thinking it has to be connected to the person who attacked him, but there's no evidence to support that."

"What about that mess at Winje's?" Remy suggested as we entered the building.

"Again, no evidence to connect that to anything. No hits on the fingerprints or the DNA." I opened the door and started climbing the stairs, Remy right behind me.

"You know," he said when we got to the top, "even if Haywire didn't actually shoot the guy, he did smack him with the barrel of the gun, didn't he? And what if he did manage to shoot him, shouldn't there be a slug somewhere? I'd think a bullet that size would've gone clean through the guy." Not waiting for a reply, he entered the room and sat at his usual place on the far side of the enormous table.

Stunned that I hadn't considered either of those possibilities, I followed and sat next to him. My mind began racing, thinking of what seemed a million things at once. It suddenly stopped when Remy nudged me.

"Robin's speaking to you."

"Huh?" I looked up to find everyone staring at me. "Oh sorry," I said. "What did you say?"

Robin smiled. "I said I was glad to see you came back. Did you get a chance to practice?"

"Uh, yeah sure," I lied.

"Great. Go ahead and cast on 15 to 20 stitches and then I'll show you the basic knitting stitch."

Oh way to go, Sarah! I pulled the needles out of the ball of yarn and managed to tie the slip knot onto one of them. Unsure of what to do next, I glanced around. Remy noticed and, using an extra needle, mimed what to do. As soon as I saw him loop the yarn around his thumb, I remembered how and soon had about three inches of stitches on my needle.

"Okay," Robin said, sitting down next to me. "Move that needle to your left hand and pick up the other one with your right." She placed her own project on the table in front of her. "Push the stitches toward the point but not so far they come off." She demonstrated, and I copied what she did. "As you do this, you want to keep tension on the yarn but not too tight. Push the point of the bare needle under the other one and into the first stitch, then hold it in place with the fingers of your left hand." She waited while I did that much. "Now, with your right hand, wrap the yarn counterclockwise around the back of the bare needle, coming between the two of them." Again, she demonstrated and then waited. "Now, this is the tricky part. Holding the yarn tight, take the bare needle in your right hand and pull it back just enough to slide the point around the left needle, picking up the loop you just made with the yarn and then slide the stitch off the left needle, essentially transferring it to the right one." She completed the stitch and smiled at me. I sat motionless, my eyes flitting from the knitting in her hand to the mess I held in mine and back again. "Go ahead, give it a try."

The silence enveloping the room told me everyone was watching, curious about my potential to succeed—or not. "Can you show me that last part one more time?"

"Certainly," she said. Robin quickly repeated the first two steps, and then stopped. "Do this part with me. Pull the point of the right one around the left one." She paused, watching me do that much. "Good. Now, push it up into the loop." Pause. "And slide the stitch off."

Using more concentration than I ever did on the shooting range, I completed the stitch.

"Wouldja look at that, she's knitting," Remy said, followed by chuckles of approval from the rest of the group. With growing confidence, I attempted a second stitch. "Push through the loop to the back..."

"That's right," Robin said.

"Take the yarn around..."

"Yes."

"Slide around, push up and off." Another stitch appeared on the needle in my right hand. "You've got it. Now, keep going and when you get to the end, I'll show you how to make the turn."

I nodded as I began stitch number three, and conversations around the table resumed. "Through the loop...push up...and off," became my mantra as I painstakingly moved the yarn from one needle to the other. So pleased with my accomplishment of completing the first row, I looked up and was immediately depressed. Knitting so quickly that it was difficult to see what their fingers were actually doing, the others chatted away as their needles clicked together like the sound of some strange insect.

"Mmm, is that jasmine tea?" Eloise asked Herb as he filled a cup from the thermos that had been sitting in front of him.

"Why, yes it is," he said.

"Ready?" Robin asked me when she noticed I'd finished.

I nodded slowly, not sure if I actually wanted to continue.

"I thought so," Eloise said, "it's one of my favorites. Do you drink tea often?"

"Prefer it to coffee actually," Herb said, "especially in the morning. Nothing like a cup of strong black tea with milk and sugar."

Robin moved down the side of the table and stood next to me. "Put down the empty needle and transfer the one with the yarn to your left hand. Now, pick up the empty one with your right hand and begin again."

"That's it?" I asked.

She laughed. "Yeah, that's it. Just watch that you don't grab the little short piece of yarn by mistake." She pointed at the one hanging from the end of my creation.

"So you've never tried it Russian style?" Eloise asked.

"I beg your pardon!" The room instantly got quiet. Even from across the table, I could see Herb's face turning red.

"She means your tea," Marjorie said without looking up.

"Oh m-m-my," Herb stammered. "Uh no, I don't believe I have."

"Add a spoonful of your favorite jam," Eloise explained. "I like raspberry in mine. Delicious."

"That does sound good. I'll have to give it a try."

"I don't go for any of that sweet stuff," Marjorie said. "To me, best cup of tea is Earl Grey with lemon."

Somehow that doesn't surprise me. I reached the end of the second row, swapped needles in my hands and began row three, slightly picking up speed.

"You know, Herb, you should come to our next Ladies' Tea Group meeting."

"What exactly happens at a tea group meeting?" he asked.

Eloise placed her knitting on the table and gave the man her full attention. "Well, we talk about tea, its history and different varieties we've tried. Sometimes we talk about books or movies. It really depends on what the hostess suggests. There's always something good to eat like finger sandwiches, scones, and sweet pastries."

"Sounds very intriguing," Herb said.

"Oh, I almost forgot. Each member brings her..." She stopped and smiled. "...or his own cup."

"Wouldn't be appropriate," Marjorie said, still focused on her knitting.

"What wouldn't be appropriate?" Eloise asked.

"Having a man attend." Marjorie stopped and rested her hands on the table.

"Why not?" I asked. *Sometimes I just can't help myself.*

Remy nudged me with his foot under the table, and I assumed he'd gotten to know the real Marjorie during knitting class.

"Well, if you must know young woman," she said, turning her intense glare on me. "In all the years the Ladies' Tea Group has met, there has never been a man in attendance and..."

Herb actually flinched and slunk down in his seat. "Well then, perhaps..."

"Now Marjorie," Eloise interrupted as she picked up her project and continued knitting. "Are you forgetting that it is my turn to host this month, and I believe I can invite anyone I want to."

"Now see here..."

"So, Eloise," Shellie said, cutting Marjorie off. "How did your event go at the library last week?"

Marjorie grunted, and I could see the slightest hint of a smile on Eloise's face as she again placed her knitting on the table. "It was a good turnout considering the weather. I had several people lined up to read stories to the children, and some of the mothers provided refreshments. I had a couple of craft things for them to do that they seemed to enjoy."

"That's nice," Shellie said. "I was going to stop by but spent most of the day shoveling snow, so that by the afternoon I was tired and ready for a nap."

"The only frustrating thing about the whole day was that my phone charger went missing," Eloise said. "True it was my old one, but it was rather convenient having one there in case I need it. Texting with my nieces and nephews can run my battery down rather quickly."

"Oh dear, do you think someone stole it?" Abigail asked.

"I don't think so; I knew almost everyone there. One of the mothers probably just moved it when they set out the refreshments on my desk. I'm sure it will turn up."

"You said you knew almost everyone. Who was there that you didn't recognize?" I asked.

"Oh, a very nice young man who said he was here visiting his grandmother, but he just sat in the corner by the window the whole time, reading magazines."

"Well, I had something weird happen the other day," Mabel said. "We've kept a couple sleeping bags in the camper shell of our truck for years, and when I went to put groceries back there this week, they were gone. I thought maybe Harold had used them for something but he said he hadn't."

"I can add to that," Bonnie said. "There's been an old lounger on the porch of the BLM office for as long as I've worked there. Not sure who it even belonged too, but Wednesday I had to stop by the office, and it was gone. I just figured either whoever owned it took it home or it finally got thrown away because it was so worn out. But now...who knows what happened to it."

I set my knitting aside and as I was pulling out the notebook and pen I'd brought "just in case," Remy nudged me with his foot again. When I looked up, his eyes were as wide as I'd ever seen them. "What in tarnation is going on here?"

"I was just wondering that myself." I flipped to a blank page and jotted down what the ladies sitting around the table had shared. "So Eloise, when was that event at the library?" I asked.

"Tuesday afternoon."

"And Mabel, the sleeping bags were missing on..."

"Well, I noticed they were gone yesterday but I hadn't used the truck in nearly a month. Only used it because it had snowed, and we never lock the camper shell, so no telling how long they've been missing."

"And Bonnie, you said the lounger was missing on Wednesday?"

She nodded. "Yeah, that's right."

I finished writing down the information for each missing item and then flip back through my notebook. *Seven items missing in the last week can hardly be a coincidence, not to mention cut brake lines and bloody vandalism.* "There has got to be something going on here," I said to Remy as I tucked my notebook and pen back into my pocket.

"You got that right!"

CHAPTER 13

I rolled over and looked at the glowing red numbers on the digital clock again. Barely an hour had passed since I last checked, and it was still way too early to be awake on a day off. However, my brain just wouldn't shut down, not even for one minute. The things Remy had said last evening and the list of suddenly missing items simply couldn't be ignored. "Maybe I *ought* to go back up to that mine," I said to my canine companion who seemed to have no problem sleeping in. As I lay supine on my bed, staring at the ceiling, I considered the options available to get there until one I'd forgotten all about popped into my head. "Pete!" I exclaimed, startling Bubbles as I sprang into a sitting position. Looking at the clock one last time, I decided it was too early to call him, so I threw back the covers, which further irritated the small dog, and began planning my day.

By the time I had the coffee brewing, Bubbles was standing by the backdoor, whining to be let out. While he did his business, I ran down to the barn to feed the horses, stopping at my patrol unit on the way back to grab my evidence case.

Killing time before I could make a phone call, I made my bed, built a fire and then made a list of what needed to be done and the supplies I'd need. At seven o'clock sharp, I dialed Pete's number.

"Howdy, Sarah."

"Hi, Pete. So...got any plans for today?" I asked.

"Nothing past making some coffee this early."

"Well, I was just wondering if you'd like to go for a snowmobile ride."

"You betcha! Have anywhere in mind?" I quickly explained my plan. "How far is it?" he asked.

"About ten miles."

"No problemo. I'll top off both tanks and be there in about an hour."

"Perfect," I said, and we disconnected.

I opened my evidence case and laid out the swabs, swab boxes, and disposable vials of distilled water I needed to secure blood samples into two piles. The first one I slid to the side—it was for the barrel of Haywire's gun. The second one needed a little preparation, so I didn't have to do it at the cabin. Using a Sharpie from my case, I wrote the date and location where I hoped to find a slug on the swab box. Then I did the same thing on a small, plastic evidence bag that would hold the slug after I'd collected whatever blood evidence it might have. I removed the digital camera from my case as well as a large pair of tweezers, a pair of gloves and a large Manila envelope to hold everything and added it to the pile. That done, I needed something to transport everything to the mine and back. If I had been traveling by horseback, I would have pulled out my saddlebags, but since I would be straddling something other than my horse, I needed to find an alternative. Not sure of what I might have, I headed to the place where all things odd or unnecessary end up—the closet in the back bedroom.

As I left the kitchen, I heard scratching at the backdoor, but given Bubble's reaction the last time I got into that closet, I left him outside. After a quick search, I found something suitable at the back of the top shelf—a small

Green Bay Packers backpack I must've purchased the same time I bought the oversized T-shirt I use as a nightshirt. I carried it out to the kitchen table and packed up the pile of supplies I'd need for collecting evidence at the mine. Then I let the persistent pooch inside and poured some dog food into his empty whipped topping bowl, hoping that would keep him occupied until I finished.

I retrieved Haywire's gun from the desk in my office and, after double-checking to make sure it was unloaded, propped it up so I could swab the barrel. While those dried, I put on my cold-weather gear sans handgun and was waiting for the toaster to eject a couple of Pop-Tarts when my cell phone rang. Recognizing the caller ID, I answered. "Hi, Sal."

"It ain't Sal. It's me Haywire. I done borrowed her phone to call you."

"Everything okay?"

"Well, here's the deal. Heard someone going through my truck last night, but they was gone before I could get out there. I'd appreciate it if I could get my gun back."

I hesitated but still could not think of any legal reason not to return the Colt .45. "I have to do something this morning but could meet you at Goose Creek later today. It's about 14 miles north of Cedarville on County Road 1. There's a ranch nearby that should give us a place to pull over."

"That seems fair," he said.

"Okay, I'll call you when I get back."

"Much obliged." He hung up.

I stuffed the dried blood samples into the swab box and placed it in the fridge. Then I poured myself another cup of coffee and looked out the kitchen window as I nibbled on one of my Pop-Tarts, wishing it was a breakfast burrito or biscuits and gravy. I'd just finished when Pete pulled down my driveway. He made a sweeping turn and ended up parking between my vehicles and the bathhouse.

"Hey Pete," I called as I stepped through the front door.

"Howdy," he replied. He had on his racing gear again but had added an insulated jacket. "You all set?"

"Think so."

He walked back to the hitch and pulled a pin just under the platform of the trailer. "This will let the trailer tip, making it easier to load and unload."

"Uh-huh." I waited until he climbed onto the trailer and then added, "Got the keys?"

"Oh that's right, you're just so damn funny."

"Nice of you to say so."

He scowled at me and then fired up the first snowmobile. I was about to ask if he planned on jumping it off the trailer when he drove it backwards.

"Reverse?" I yelled over the sound of the engine. "It has reverse?"

When he cleared the trailer, he pulled up next to me. "Yeah, isn't it cool." He cut the motor and climbed off. "There are a couple helmets on the front passenger seat if you wanna grab 'em while I get the other one unloaded."

"Sure thing." As I placed a helmet on the seat of each snowmobile, Pete pointed toward my driveway and said, "Who's that?"

I turned around. "That's Remy."

"What on earth is he riding?"

"That would be his John Deere snowmobile."

"You rode that for ten miles?"

"Twenty, if you count the trip back."

We watched as my neighbor continued down the driveway and parked next to us. "Thought that was you that drove by," Remy said after shutting off the engine.

"Where did you get that antique?" Pete asked.

Ignoring the question, Remy continued. "Thought maybe you were figuring on riding on up the road here. If so, I'd be happy to show you a few of the sights." He was already dressed in his snowsuit and Elmer Fudd hat.

"Actually Remy," I said, "we're going back up to the cabin at Moonlight Mine."

"What in tarnation do you want to go back up there for?"

"Well, what you said last night got me thinking, so I've decided to look for the slug."

"Then I guess you could use another pair of eyes." He turned the key on. "I can be ready in a jiffy." He pulled on the cord and the snowmobile fired up. "Bring Bubba on over to my place," he hollered over the sound of the engine, "and he can hang out with Millie while we're gone." He started to pull away but stopped. "You ought maybe have Sarah practice a bit before starting out. She's not exactly the best snowmobile rider." Then he headed back toward his place.

Pete looked at me. "What did he mean by that?"

During my explanation as to why I didn't want to go for a snowmobile ride the previous weekend, I failed to include the part about tipping over while making a turn.

"Come on," Pete coaxed. "If there's some kind of problem with you riding snowmobiles, I need to know. These aren't mine, remember."

"Fine. When I was trying to ride Remy's, it kept tipping over when I tried to turn."

Pete stood there looking at me for a few seconds, and then he burst out laughing. "You mean...you fell off!"

And there it is! A few months ago, I was riding Raven around Fee Reservoir when he suddenly spooked, causing me to lose my seat and hit the ground. To make matters worse, my horse then decided to run off and leave me stranded. Pete just happened to be in the area riding his dirt bike and was able to stop the runaway. Since then, he has enjoyed teasing me about falling off my horse every chance he gets.

I folded my arms across my chest and gave him my best deputy glare. "I told you, it tipped over. You saw how narrow it is and how high the seat is."

"Come on, then. We better see if you can keep one of these on its skis." He moved the helmet off the seat of the closest snowmobile. "Get on." While I climbed aboard, he unclipped one end of a curly, red cord and hooked it to the zipper of my jacket. "This is connected to the kill switch, so the machine can't get away from you when you fall off."

"Gee, thanks," I said.

"The controls are a lot like a motorcycle or ATV. The brake is here on the left along with the reverse button, but you don't need to worry about that. On the right here, you've got the main switch, which needs to be in the RUN position. Operate the accelerator with your thumb, and first start of the day, you'll want to flip up the choke here on the center console all the way." Pete demonstrated. "It's electronic start, so just turn the key to start it."

I did, and it fired right up.

Pete leaned in. "Let it smooth out," he said. In less than a minute, it was running great, so I flipped the choke switch back down.

"Now, the most important thing to remember when you turn is..."

"I know...lean."

"Well, actually it's more of a slide. You want to keep your center of gravity as low as possible, so kinda hang a cheek off the seat as you lean."

"Hang a cheek?" I asked, looking up at him.

He shrugged. "Give it a try."

I pressed on the accelerator and rode toward the barn. When I reached the driveway, I turned the handlebar to the left, slid my left cheek off the seat, and leaned. The snowmobile turned—and I stayed on.

Pete started jumping up and down, pumping his right fist over his head as I rode back. When I got closer, he began waving his right hand in a circular motion. I nodded in acknowledgement and repeated a left-hand turn and headed back toward the barn. This time I veered left and executed a right-hand turn successfully. Feeling quite confident, I sped back toward him and stopped.

"Looks like you pass," Pete said, his crystal-blue eyes twinkling at me. He pressed on the main switch and shut down the engine. "Ready to go?"

"Let me grab my supplies and lock up the house." I bailed off and went inside. I put on my backpack and grabbed my gloves. After securing the backdoor, I scooped up Bubbles and exited through the front door, locking it behind me.

Pete, wearing his own backpack and one of the helmets, sat on the other idling machine. "Here, I'll take the dog, since I've had more practice riding one-handed."

I passed the miniature mutt over, pulled on the remaining helmet, and got on. As soon as I started the engine, Pete took off with Bubbles perched on the seat in front of him with his front paws resting on the console. Moments later, we parked next to the John Deere, knocked and went inside. Bubbles wiggled out of Pete's arms to greet the small white goat, and the two them ran off to another part of the house.

Remy was in the kitchen dumping ingredients into his bread machine. "Got me a stew in the crockpot. Turned it on low so it won't stick and burn by the time we get back.

This here loaf of bread can cool in the pan." He closed the lid and pressed the start button. "Oh, I almost forgot." He opened the freezer section of his refrigerator and removed a square, foil-covered pan, put it into the oven and set the temperature.

"What's that?" I asked.

Remy's grin bloomed under his white beard and trimmed mustache. "Never you mind. That there's a surprise." He pulled back on the buffalo plaid hat he'd tossed onto the table. "Ready?"

"You betcha," Pete said.

"You two behave yourselves," Remy called over his shoulder as he pulled the door closed.

We fired up the snowmobiles and with Remy on point, headed up Highgrade Road. The first mile or so, Pete stayed behind the older machine until his patience and sense of fun could no longer tolerate what I'm sure he considered to be a snail's pace.

First he began zigzagging in front of me, riding up onto the higher embankments along the road when the opportunity arose. But when we reached the point where Haywire had to break through the berm left behind from plowing, Pete launched himself off one of them just like I'd seen him do with his dirt bike over a sagebrush, landing right next to the old John Deere before speeding away. I accelerated until I was even with Remy, about to comment on the daredevil's antics, but the expression on the old man's face clearly indicated he was not amused, so I changed my mind, and we rode for a while in silence.

Pete finally had his fill of playing and waited just before the hairpin turn for us to catch up. With Remy again in the lead, we traveled the rest of the way together, arriving at the mine a few minutes later. We followed Haywire's tracks up to the cabin and could plainly see both sets of footprints going to and from the door. The hasp had been pried loose, so getting into the cabin was easy.

"Wow," I said, stepping inside. "I had no idea it was this bad." Saltines had been strewn everywhere along with other food items that had been dumped from their containers.

"Somebody was desperately lookin for something," Pete said.

"Most likely the money," I murmured as I removed my backpack and set it on the table.

"What money?" Pete and Remy asked in unison.

I quickly explained about the payoff from the bookie in Vegas and how I suspected that it was somehow connected to what had been happening with Haywire. "In fact," I added, "he apparently kept a strong box up here full of money." I approached the wood stove and knelt down. A small section of the floor sat slightly askew.

"Under there?" Remy asked.

"That's what he told me," I said, getting to my feet. "And also why he was so determined to get back up here to retrieve it." I opened my backpack and pulled out the supplies I'd brought. "Let's spread out and look for any holes or notches in the walls or trim."

"Didn't Haywire say he was lying on the floor when he pulled the trigger?" Remy asked.

"Yeah, so the bullet may have hit high or low, depending on the angle."

We'd only been searching for a few minutes when Remy called me into the storage room where he'd located newspaper to start a fire the last time we were there. "There's a chunk of wood missing from this shelf," he said. "I looked under here but it's too dark to see."

I unzipped my jacket, pulled my phone from the pocket of my fleece pullover, and pressed the flashlight app.

Leaning in, I examined the hole in the wall. "I think that's what we're looking for." I retrieved my digital camera and took a couple pictures. "Should be able to dig it out with my knife," I said, reaching for my pocket, but I wasn't wearing my uniform; therefore, no pockets and no knife. "Pete, got a knife I can use?"

"You betcha." He reached for it but then stopped, experiencing the same problem I did. Shrugging, he gave me a sheepish grin.

Remy chuckled. "Guess them newfangled duds are missing a few essential parts." He unzipped his snowsuit, removed the Case pocketknife from the jeans he had on underneath, and handed it over.

"Thanks." I slid my upper body onto the shelf and managed to loosen the slug. "Somebody hand me those tweezers and that small plastic bag off the table," I called, reaching my left hand behind me. As soon as I had the slug secured, I sat down at the table to process it. "This will just take a few minutes."

"So, what are you hoping to discover?" Pete asked.

"Some kinda connection between the fella that attacked Haywire and that mess at Winje's."

Pete turned to me. "What mess?"

"Looked like somebody broke into their cabin last weekend," I said, moistening the tip of a swab.

"Got blood all over the place," Remy added.

"Blood?" Pete looked from Remy to me. "From what?"

"Haywire thinks he smacked whoever attacked him with his gun and then shot him," Remy reported.

"He managed to fire a shot but doesn't know if he hit the guy or not," I corrected. I propped the damp swab I'd used on the slug against the box to dry and dropped the slug back into the small evidence bag. "So, by swabbing the barrel of his gun and this," I said, holding it up, "we might have enough to compare to the samples I took at Winje's and verify whether or not it's the same person."

"And if it is?" Pete asked.

I shrugged. "At first, I figured he was long gone, but now I'm not so sure."

"Because..."

"It's a long story," I said, securing everything to go to Josh at the lab in the Manila envelope and sealing it.

"And one we can tell over bread and stew when we get back," Remy said.

"I need to meet up with Haywire as soon as we get back to return his gun." I packed up the rest of my stuff into the backpack and pulled it into place. "But that shouldn't take long."

"Well then, if you're done..." Remy said to me, and I nodded. "...let's head on outta here."

Securing the door behind us as best as we could, we fired up the snowmobiles and headed back. Pete, of course, raced ahead, riding up onto the banks of the road and jumping over anything he could find. Feeling more confident myself, I began following him up the smaller embankments and even went over a jump—once.

Remy, however, refused to budge from the center of the road. That is, until Pete had ridden around a corner out of sight, and I was heading from one bank across the road to another. I happened to look over my shoulder just in time to see him veer to the right and go up onto the bank, nearly tipping over in the process, and back down the other side. I never saw him make any other attempts, but I had to give him credit for giving it a try.

It was around noon when Remy rode into his place, and we continued on down my driveway. "Go ahead and take off," Pete said after we pulled up behind the trailer. "I'll take care of loading these and then walk over to Remy's."

I dashed into the house and grabbed the Colt .45 and the keys to my Ford Dooley. As I pulled out onto County Road 1, I called Sal's cell phone. Haywire answered on the second ring and informed me he was heading out as soon as we hung up.

The drive south was uneventful. With no additional snowfall since Wednesday, door yards and driveways were already cleared and snowmobiles had other more exciting places to play than on a county road. I reached the designated meeting spot ahead of Haywire, so I pulled off and waited.

The line of willows accentuated by the layer of snow made it easy to follow the path of Goose Creek where almost a year ago I'd worked on my first real case as deputy. Gus Miller, a man who kept primarily to himself and was thought to have left the area a few months before, was found where the creek dumps into Upper Lake. Apparently, he'd been caught in a huge flash flood and washed downstream from the base of Buck Mountain where I later located his car and the remains of his dog. But before I could reminisce any further, I caught sight of the rust over light blue Dodge Power Wagon. It pulled in next to me, and Haywire climbed out.

"Sure appreciate this," he said when he walked up to the window I'd just rolled down. "Things is getting a might hazardous around here."

I opened the cylinder of the revolver and handed it over. "Just remember this is for self-defense. Don't go looking for trouble."

"Never do." He looked the gun over before clicking the cylinder back into place. "But when it comes lookin' for me, I like to be ready."

That's what I'm afraid of. "And give me a call if anything else weird happens."

"Will do." He started back toward his truck. "Much obliged," he said, waving the gun over his head.

I waited for him to pull out before starting the engine and driving back toward Fort Bidwell. As I traveled north, large dark clouds began drifting over the Warners and into Surprise Valley, blotting out the sun.

A few minutes later, I parked in front of Remy's and got out. A light snow had begun to fall, and I paused at the base of the stairs for a moment, enjoying the quiet. Greeted by the smell of fresh baked bread and beef stew and the sounds of the Highway Men as I stepped through the front door, I suddenly felt like I'd come home.

CHAPTER 14

He punched in his PIN number on the pad, selected his checking account, and then the amount of the withdrawal. The ATM beeped and an error message flashed on the screen. *Insufficient funds. Account balance $3.22.* "Dammit. That's all I need." He yanked his debit card out of the slot and trudged off through the falling snow, his feet freezing in the soaked tennis shoes. Passing between two cars parked in the front of the small market, he glanced inside the one on his right and stopped. "I think my luck is about to change."

I shut off the alarm and rolled over onto my back. Feeling more rested and relaxed than I had in weeks, I lay in bed for a little while longer, thinking about how nice the day before had been.

Pete had ended up staying the night, and we awoke to heavy snowfall which had added several more inches overnight. After a breakfast of Apple Brown Betty leftover from dinner the night before, we spent most of the day huddled up in front of the wood stove, watching movies. When the snow finally stopped, Pete unhooked the snowmobile trailer, with a promise to come back and get it after the roads had been plowed, and headed home. I spent the rest of the day clearing paths and making sure the horses had plenty of food and water.

Early to bed last night, I was anxious to begin a new work week.

I threw back the covers, but as soon as my feet hit the floor, my cell phone went off. *Now what?* I grabbed it off the charger and answered. "Murdock."

"Hey, Sarah. It's Ira. I just got a 911 call from the owner of High Desert Hot Springs."

"What's going on?" I asked, following Bubbles to the backdoor.

"Some guy just showed up there almost froze to death, claiming his wife and baby are stuck in their vehicle somewhere off the end of Highway 299."

"What the heck are they doing out there this time of year?"

"I've got no details. Only that the guy is frantic to go get them."

"Copy that. I'll throw on my uniform and head that way. Have you got any rescue vehicles rolling?"

"Not yet. Called you first."

"Okay. See what's available, and I'll contact you after I get there and figure out what's going on."

"On it." And he hung up.

I let the dog back in and dressed as quickly as I could. Not wanting to waste time explaining the situation to Remy, I grabbed my jacket and portable radio, picked up Bubbles and dashed out the front door.

Road conditions prevented me from traveling much over 40 miles per hour, so I didn't reach the resort until after the sun had poked its head over the Hays Canyon Range, which runs along the eastern edge of Surprise Valley. "Okay, Dog." Bubbles looked up from his spot on the front seat. "You stay here until I find out just what's going on." As soon as I climbed out of my patrol unit, Abigail burst out the front door and herded me inside.

Entering the small parlor furnished with nineteenth century antiques was like stepping into a sauna. The small box stove had been thoroughly stoked and was practically glowing. A young man in his late twenties was wrapped in two quilts and seated right next to it in one of the oak chairs. A second oak chair, wearing what I assumed was his jacket, sat next to him.

"Dear," Abigail began, "this is Zach." The man turned toward me. "Zach, this is Deputy..."

"Thank God you're here!" he exclaimed, leaping to his feet. The quilts fell apart just enough for me to realize he didn't have much else on. "We've got to go save Jenny and the baby. There was only a quarter of a tank of gas when I left, and it's so cold."

"Now, hold on a minute," I said, placing a hand on his shoulder and applying enough pressure to make him sit back down. "I'll check on the rescue vehicles in a second, but first I need some more information. Can you tell me where exactly your car..."

"It's a truck," Zach interrupted. "A red Nissan Frontier."

"Okay. And where is it?"

The young man sat silent for a moment. "I'm not sure. We'd stopped in Cedar...Cedar..."

"Cedarville," Abigail said, smiling at him.

He nodded. "Cedarville, and we got gas. Must've been around four o'clock. By five, we'd slid off the road and into the ditch. We didn't have cell service, so we tried digging ourselves out, but even with the truck in four-wheel drive, we couldn't do it. Then it started snowing, so we got back inside to keep warm and waited for someone to come by and help us."

"But it started snowing on Saturday," I said.

Zach nodded again. "Yeah, we left our house around noon on Saturday. The next morning, I wanted to go for help, but Jenny didn't want me walking around during the storm. She was afraid I'd get lost, but when we'd burned through most of the tank of gas, I insisted I go for help."

"Where were you heading?" I asked.

"We were following Highway 299 to get to Burns, Oregon."

"But that doesn't..." Ed Flowers began but stopped when I looked at him and slightly shook my head.

"Okay," I continued, "and do you know how far you had traveled before you got stuck?"

"Not really. It was getting dark and we couldn't go very fast. All I know it's that I've been walking since ten o'clock last night, and we've got to go get my family before the damn truck runs out of gas!"

I turned to Abigail. "What time did he show up here?"

"Oh my. What time was it Ed?" she asked her husband.

"I'd say it was about six."

I counted on my fingers. "So, it took him about eight hours to get here. And what was the road like? Could you walk very fast?"

"Deep snow, up past my knees or deeper in some places."

"I'd say he started out about 12 to 15 miles from here," Ed said.

"That's what I was thinking." I pulled out my cell phone and called dispatch.

"Sheriff's Office." It was Cindy.

"Cindy, it's Sarah. Did Ira fill you in?"

"Sure did. How are things out there?"

"Apparently, we do have a rescue. Young woman and a baby stranded in a Nissan truck about 12 to 15 miles off the end of 299. Any ETA on those rescue vehicles?"

"Just got an update. The ambulance is on the way but

it looks like the grader won't even reach your location for at least another hour, maybe two."

"Two hours?"

"Two hours!" Zach sprang to his feet again. "No way! We've got to get to them sooner than that." He turned to Abigail. "Where are my clothes? I need my clothes!"

"You sit back down, Dear, and I'll go check on them." She nodded at Ed as she left the room, and he encouraged Zach to sit back down.

"Keep me posted," I told Cindy. "And you might see if your uncle is available. We may need a tow truck to pull the vehicle out."

"You bet." We disconnected.

If only the snowmobiles were closer, maybe we could... Then it hit me—the tank! I immediately dialed Sal's number and stepped out into the entryway. She finally answered on the tenth ring.

"Hi Sal, it's Sarah," I said before she even had a chance to say anything. "I need to speak with Haywire."

"Well, he's a sittin' right here having breakfast."

"Great, put him on."

"Howdy," he said a moment later.

"I've got a situation and could really use your help." I quickly explained what was going on and asked, "Do you think your truck can get there?"

"Don't see why not. I'm leaving right now."

He hung up, and I slipped my phone back into my pocket as I returned to the parlor. "I may have a way to reach them sooner."

"Really?" Zach said, poking his head around the quilt Ed and Abigail had been holding up as a makeshift privacy screen.

"Yeah. I know someone with a four-wheel-drive truck with chains."

Zach finished dressing and stepped out from behind the screen, which was quickly folded up and tossed on the small lounging couch. "How long 'til we leave?"

"I expect he'll be here in less than half an hour. But you're not going," I told him.

"Whatd'ya mean I'm not going?"

"There's only room for three in the cab. Besides, I think Ed should drive you into Cedarville and have you checked out at the emergency room."

"But there's nothing wrong with me," he protested.

"Just as a precaution. Then you'll already be there when we bring your family in." I turned to Ed. "Do you by chance have a can of gas I could take with us?"

"I think I might have some out in the shed."

"Great. Not knowing how much is left in their vehicle, I'd hate to have it run out as they are trying to bring it back. The other thing," I added, speaking to Abigail, "is my dog. I didn't have time to drop him off, so would you mind looking after him until we get back."

"Where is he now?" she asked.

"Out in the Explorer."

"Oh heavens, he's probably freezing out there. Bring him in right away, and I'll make a place for him right by the stove." She bustled out of the room.

After stepping out to my patrol unit, I pulled on my jacket and grabbed my radio along with the first aid kit out of the back, just in case. Then I gathered up the sleeping dog and met Ed at the door. He was carrying a jerry can filled with gas, which he left on the step. Back inside, I dropped Bubbles at my feet and ushered him into the parlor.

"This is your dog?" Abigail asked. "I thought it belonged to your sister."

"Long story. But, he's mine now."

"Well, come on over here and get warm," Abigail said to Bubbles.

The dog looked at me and then at Abigail before trotting over and curling up on a blanket she'd put down on the floor for him. *Good grief!* As soon as he was settled, Abigail left the room.

"Well, you might as well head in with Zach," I said to Ed. "I'm sure the guy with the truck will be here shortly." I walked with the two of them toward the door. "As soon as I know anything, I'll radio dispatch and have them call the hospital and let you know what's going on."

"I'd really appreciate that," Zach said as I followed them out to Ed's dark grey GMC truck.

Looking out toward the highway, I saw Haywire make the turn and head up the driveway. Zach must have seen it too, because he climbed back down out of the the passenger seat and came over to where I was standing.

"That can't be the truck you're talking about," he began. "Look at it. It looks like it's about to fall apart."

"Don't let how it looks fool you. That thing is a tank in the snow and very well maintained." *Oh brother, now I sound just like Haywire!*

"I still say I ought to go with you, especially if you're going in that."

"I told you there isn't enough room. Now go on," I urged, leading him back to Ed's truck, "and wait for my call." He climbed back in, and I closed his door.

The two rigs passed each other at the end of the driveway, and Haywire pulled up next to me, leaned over, and rolled down the passenger window. "You ready?" he called.

"Just about. There's a can of gas on the step. If you'll load it into the bed of your truck, I'll go grab my first aid kit." I went back inside and met Abigail in the entryway.

"Oh, good. I thought you'd already left." She handed over a small paper bag and a thermos. "A couple banana nut muffins and some milk. I'm sure that nursing mother is starving right about now. I also want to send along those two quilts to keep both of them warm on the trip back." She hustled into the parlor and retrieved them and my first aid kit. "Go on ahead and I'll carry these." She followed me out to the truck and waited until I was settled in the passenger seat before handing over the items she was holding. "Now, you tell Ed when you see him that he's to bring that little family back here to stay until their vehicle is ready for them to continue on their way."

"I will, Abigail. Thanks. Now get back inside where it's warm." She turned away, and I rolled up the window. "All right," I said to Haywire, "let's get this rescue started."

He coaxed the Dodge Power Wagon into first gear and steered it down the driveway. Turning right, we headed east on Highway 299.

CHAPTER 15

"How far in did you say this rig we're looking for is?" Haywire asked as he downshifted and we left the plowed section of 299. Faint indentations indicated the passing of a vehicle prior to the latest dump of fresh snow the day before.

"We're thinking the husband walked 12 to 15 miles, and we've already come at least four, so I'm guessing they traveled up into here ten miles or so before getting stuck."

Haywire checked his odometer. "Last two numbers read 23, so if we get to 40 and haven't spotted it, we may have to do some exploring. But judging by those," he said nodding at a set of footprints in the groove on the left, "I think we're on the right track."

I had to agree—as long as we could still make out the indentations of the tire tracks, but when Haywire guided the Power Wagon up a long rise, they disappeared under a snowdrift. The footprints, however, continued up and over the large mound of snow.

"Now what?" I asked.

"Won't know 'til I check it out." He exited the truck and tromped through the snow toward the drift. He walked along the edge and climbed up on it in a couple places before returning to the truck. "Not as deep along that right side," he said, putting the truck in gear, "and there doesn't appear to be any big rocks that could hang us up." Haywire slowly released the clutch and veered to the right. The Dodge tipped as the driver's side crawled over the edge of the drift, but he skillfully guided that tank of his past the drift and back onto the road, where we again followed the slight indentations of tire tracks dotted with footprints.

With major landmarks buried under the layer of snow as well as the reflection of bright sunlight, I was having trouble figuring out where exactly we were until he let me know we'd driven five miles. Then I was able to recognize the wide area to the left where I'd parked my horse trailer during one of my training sessions with Raven the previous fall.

We continued to climb up the western slope of the range, but just before reaching the summit, we encountered another snowdrift so enormous it extended to the right for several yards past the edge of the road. The trail of footprints veered to the left and disappeared into a cluster of juniper trees, which formed a natural barricade.

"Looks like I'm walking from here," I said.

"No telling how much further that rig might be," Haywire pointed out.

"That's true, but it could just be around the next bend, and I won't know for sure unless I check it out."

"Well..." He sat looking out the windshield. "You see how it's all flat out that way," he said, nodding to the right.

"Yes."

"Could be that's good solid ground under that snow."

"Even though it's on an incline?"

"Oh sure. A good running start, we'd have no problem getting up that."

I thought about what Haywire was proposing. If everything went as planned, we'd be able to continue, locate the vehicle and get the mother and baby back to

Cedarville. Worst case scenario, we get stuck but could still continue on foot and at least bring them food, gas and blankets to keep them warm until other help arrived. "Okay, let's go for it."

"Alrighty, but first we need to go walk that area and make sure there are no surprises. Hard to tell with all this glare." He shut down the engine, and we got out. Within a short amount of time, we'd determined there were no hidden ditches to rip off a wheel and where we'd have to leave and reenter the road were clear of any obstacles.

"Here we go," Haywire said, firing up the engine after we'd climbed back into the cab of the Power Wagon. He backed up a short distance, dropped it into first gear, and began our run. Carefully accelerating, he shifted to second gear as we left the roadway and maneuvered around the snowdrift. Climbing up the hillside, I grabbed for the dashboard as we bounced over the rough terrain.

"Yahoo," he exclaimed when we burst back onto the road and came to a stop. I let out a huge sigh, completely unaware I'd been holding my breath.

We continued up the hill and by the time we reached the top, my heart rate was almost back to normal. Haywire downshifted, and we headed down the steep slope on the other side. "Best to let the tranny hold us back and keep off the brakes. That's when most folks get into trouble."

"I see what you mean," I said, pointing at the zig-zag pattern the partially buried tire tracks had left on the road in front of us. "I think we're getting close." Creeping along, we followed the tracks, which alternated between moving in a straight line and zig-zagging from one side of the road to the other; the footprints traveled along the center. The road began to level out as we entered a sharp turn to the left, and I spotted the truck nose first in a ditch. "There it is!"

Haywire stopped directly behind it. "You go check on them whilst I find a place to get turned around."

I grabbed my first aid kit and one of the quilts and bailed out. Hurrying toward the passenger side of the truck, I hung onto the side of it as I made my way into the ditch. Approaching the window, I could see the head of the occupant leaning against it, but she gave no indication that she'd heard our arrival. Not wanting to startle her, I gently tapped on the glass.

She instantly sat up and turned to look over her shoulder, an expression of terror contorting her face. It soon melted into tears of relief when she realized I was there to rescue her.

"Oh thank God," she sobbed opening her door. As she swiveled in her seat, I saw the tiny head of the baby nestled inside her coat.

"My name's Sarah," I told her.

"Jenny. I was so scared no one was going to come. Is Zach okay?"

"He's just fine and very anxious to see you. Can you stand?"

"Yes, I think so." She scooted toward the door, pulling the sleeping bag she'd wrapped around the two of them along with her.

"Here." I put the first aid kit in the snow at my feet and slightly opened the quilt. "This is nice and warm. Hand me the baby so you can get out." Reluctantly, she opened her coat and handed the child over. I quickly folded the quilt around it and held it tight against my chest. "Grab just the essentials. We need to get both of you out of this ditch and up to the road.

The woman stuffed a few things into the backpack on the floor and then reached for the keys hanging from the ignition.

"Best to leave those for whoever comes to get the truck. They'll need them in order to drive it back once they get it back on the road."

"Of course." She stepped out. "Oh, what about the car seat?"

"There's only room for us in the cab."

"I see. Well..." She wrapped the sleeping bag around her shoulders, and picked up the backpack. "Ready."

"You go ahead, and I'll be right behind you," I said.

She looked at the bundle in my arms and frowned. "Are you sure?"

"Absolutely."

Slowly, she turned and started up the bank toward the road, struggling a couple of times to stay on her feet. I followed, again holding onto the bed of the truck with my free hand, so I wouldn't do the same. Finally, we reached the road.

"Where's your vehicle?" Jenny asked, looking first one direction and then the other.

"I'm sure Haywire will be along shortly."

"Haywire?"

I nodded. "His real name is Henry. He just had to find a place to turn around."

Minutes ticked by. The woman pulled the sleeping bag around her more tightly and stomped her sneaker-clad feet. "I'm getting cold. Let me see how Brody's doing?" She lifted a corner of the quilt and peered into the peaceful face of her child. "Thank goodness, he's still sleeping. Maybe we should get back into the truck."

I was about to agree until I heard the sound of a vehicle approaching. *Finally!*

Seconds later, Haywire's rust over light blue truck came into sight, and Jenny looked at me with the same scared look I'd seen when I rapped on her window.

I smiled and shook my head. "No need to worry. We'll be perfectly safe."

Haywire pulled up next to us and rolled down his window. "Sorry, but I had to go a ways before I could get turned around."

"We're just glad to see you," I said. "This is Jenny. Jenny, this is Haywire."

"Pleased to meet you," she said.

"Right back at ya. Now, get in and let's get going."

I guided her around the back of the truck and opened the door. "Hand me the sleeping bag," I said, "and climb in." I draped it over the door and handed the baby to Jenny after she got settled. "There's another quilt next to you if you need it." I handed over the thermos and brown paper bag I'd placed on the dash. "There are a couple of muffins in here if you're hungry and milk in the thermos. Give me a minute to take this back," I said, gathering up the sleeping bag, "along with that can of gas, in case they need it." I shut the door and plucked the jerry can out of the bed of Haywire's truck. Without a free hand to hang on, my second trip into the ditch was a bit trickier, but I managed to stay on my feet. The can went into the snow-filled bed, and I tossed the sleeping bag into the passenger seat. Then I retrieved my first aid kit and clambered up out of the ditch.

By the time I got back in the truck, Jenny had devoured the first muffin and downed at least half of the milk, drinking it right out of the thermos. "Oh, thank you," she said in between bites, "I was so hungry."

Haywire shifted into first gear, and we began the trek back.

"Abigail thought you might be," I said, reaching for my radio. "Modoc, 113."

"Who's Abigail," Jenny asked around a mouthful of muffin.

"Go ahead, 113."

"Hang on," I said to her. Depressing the button on my radio again, I answered. "We have located the woman and baby and are bringing them back."

"Copy, 113. Good to hear."

The truck gained momentum, and Haywire shifted into second.

"You can cancel the ambulance but have the grader and tow truck continue. There are a couple of drifts that will need to be cleared, and the vehicle is in a ditch on the right hand side of the road about ten miles in. A red Nissan Frontier. It should be drivable once it's out of the ditch, so Bert may want to bring an extra body. There's a can of gas in the bed. Not sure how much is left in the tank."

"Copy, I'll let him know."

"And can you please give the hospital in Cedarville a 10-21 and have them let the husband, first of Zach, know that we're bringing them in."

"Will do. And same 10-20 for the Nissan?"

Remembering what Abigail had said, I replied, "No, have them drop it off at the High Desert Hot Springs."

"Copy. Time 9:28."

"Abigail is the owner of the place Zach managed to walk to," I said, placing my radio back on the dash. "She figured a nursing mother would be starving."

Jenny drained the thermos, handed it to me and wiped her mouth with the back of her hand. "And she was right."

The Power Wagon continued to crawl up the steep road toward the top.

"I'm curious," I began, "about how you guys ended up on this road, especially in the winter."

"Heading to my folks' place for the holidays." She lifted the edge of the quilt and checked on the baby. "They haven't seen Brody yet, and we wanted to surprise them."

"Where do your folks live?"

"Burns, Oregon."

Haywire and I exchanged glances. "But you can't get there very easily on this road," I said.

"Sure you can. My map app said to take Highway 99 from Durham to Redding, then I-5 to Highway 299, which connects with Highway 20 toward Burns."

"Not exactly. Highway 299 joins 395 in Alturas, and that's the highway that connects with 20. Highway 299 turns to the right just north of Alturas and basically ends at the edge of Surprise Valley, which is where we're headed."

"What?" Jenny exclaimed, tears forming in her eyes. "You mean it's my fault we got stuck?"

"You must've just read the route wrong," I offered.

"I didn't think so. I glanced at the map when it popped up but decided to read through the actual directions, and they said..." She stopped and placed her hand over her mouth. "Oh no," she whimpered.

"What?"

Reaching the summit, Haywire downshifted back into first gear, and we began creeping down the other side.

"The baby had started to fuss, so I closed the app and went into his room to pick him up." Tears spilled from her eyes and ran down her cheeks. "I must not have read the whole thing." She began sobbing.

"So you're from Durham?" I asked a moment later in an effort to distract her.

"Yes." She swiped at her nose with the back of her hand. "Zach's going to Butte College and working part-time. When his boss agreed to give him a couple of weeks off, we thought it would be nice to spend Christmas with family." The baby wiggled and uttered a small cry. "Shh, Brody." Jenny gently bounced him up and down. "It's okay."

"Actually, it might be good for him to be awake," I said. "Our ride is about to get a little bumpy."

"What do you mean?" she asked. Following my gaze, she looked out the windshield. "Look out!" she cried when she saw the huge snowdrift blocking the road. "Where did that come from?"

"Brace yourself," Haywire called as he veered left and drove off the road.

"What are you doing?" Jenny shouted, clutching the baby against her chest. "Are you crazy?"

"To some, I 'spect I am," he replied.

"It's all right," I said, trying to calm the young mother down. "See, we made a path when we came through the first time."

Because he was not trying to maintain momentum, Haywire was able to navigate more slowly, making the ride slightly smoother. Even so, we still got jostled around pretty good before he finally pulled back onto the roadway.

"We don't' have to do that again, do we?" Jenny asked.

"Well, actually..." Haywire began.

I quickly cut him off. "But it's nothing like that. Just a tiny detour around a much smaller drift."

"Unit 113, Modoc. Status check."

I grabbed my radio off the dash. "Modoc, 113. We are Code 4 and almost back to the valley floor. ETA at the hospital is about 45 minutes."

"Copy, 113. Code 4."

CHAPTER 16

As Haywire pulled into the same parking spot at the Surprise Valley Hospital I'd used a mere ten days ago, I glanced inside. Ed was sitting in one of the four available chairs reading the paper, and Zach was pacing back and forth. He didn't even notice that we'd arrived until we walked through the door. As soon as he spotted us, he ran to the interior door, threw it open and yelled, "They're here!" Then he darted across the waiting room and wrapped his arms around his wife and child. "Oh Jenny," he sobbed, "I'm so glad you're safe."

A wave of awkwardness rolled through the room, and the three of us did our best to avert our eyes and focus on other things in our surroundings. It ended quickly when Dr. Franny swept in.

"I had a feeling it was you," she exclaimed, smiling at me. "When this young man said a deputy had gone after his wife, I just knew it had to be you."

Nurse Emily appeared seconds later, wearing a Grinch themed scrub top this time, and rolled a wheelchair over to the little family still locked in a tight embrace. "Okay, break it up," she said. "Let's get these two checked out."

Zach reluctantly released Jenny and held Brody while she sat down. Then he handed over his son, and the nurse whisked them away.

"Be right back," Dr. Franny said, closing the door behind her.

"Thank you so much for finding them," Zach said, stepping over and shaking first Haywire's hand and then mine. "I don't know how to repay you."

"Just doing my job," I said.

"Well, if you ask me you were damn lucky. Why on earth didn't you turn around when you saw the road hadn't been plowed?" Haywire asked.

Zach took a step back and blinked a couple of times. "Well, the baby was fussing, and Jenny kept saying we were on the right road." He shrugged. "We just wanted to get to her folks' house as soon as we could."

"Well, you almost didn't get there at all!"

"Haywire," I said, stepping toward him. He glowered at the young man and took a seat next to Ed.

"I know, I know." Zach began sobbing. "And now, we don't have anywhere to stay until we get our truck back." He slumped into the nearest chair.

"Oh, that reminds me. Ed, Abigail told me to tell you to bring these people back to the resort to stay until they're ready to continue on their journey."

Zach looked up. "Really?"

"Trust me, when Abby sets her mind to something, it's just best to go along with it. That being said, looks like you're going home with me."

"Oh, thank you so much."

Before Ed could reply, the interior door banged opened again, and Emily wheeled Jenny and the baby back into the waiting room. "Here you go," she said. "Everything checked out just fine."

"Oh, I'm so glad." Zach hurried over, picked up Brody and gave him a big hug.

"If you'd like to pull whichever vehicle is giving them a

ride over to the door, I'd be happy to bring her out," Emily said.

"I can walk." Jenny started to get up.

"No, no. Hospital policy. I have to wheel you out."

"No sense fighting it," Haywire said. "You can't win." He stood and moved toward the door.

Just then, Dr. Franny stepped through the doorway. "Hang on there just a minute," she said, looking at Haywire. "I believe it's time to have that shoulder of yours checked."

"Nope." The man shrugged a couple of times and waved his left arm around. "It's just fine."

"Why don't you let me be the judge of that." Dr. Franny motioned toward Haywire for him to follow her. When he didn't move, she added, "Or I can call your friend and see what she says."

"Ain't giving you no number, so you're wasting your time."

Dr. Franny looked over at us. "Where does she work?"

While the others just kind of looked at each other, I spoke up. "Wagon Wheel Café."

If looks could kill, I would have been lying dead on the floor. But accepting the fact that he was outgunned, Haywire reluctantly followed the doctor and disappeared into the depths of the hospital.

"Well, looks like I need a ride back to my patrol unit," I said to Ed.

"Sure thing, there's plenty of room."

"Thanks. Just let me grab the rest of my stuff and Abigail's other quilt out of Haywire's truck." By the time I got to Ed's GMC, everyone else was already loaded, and Emily was pushing the wheelchair back inside where it was warm. Wondering if Haywire would also have to ride out in a wheelchair forced an involuntary giggle to erupt that I quickly disguised as a cough.

Back at the High Desert Hot Springs, I collected my dog, which I actually had to carry out because he wouldn't budge from his spot by the stove, and climbed back into the Explorer. As I let it warm up, I gave Remy a call to explain why I hadn't dropped off Bubbles.

"Heard the chatter on the scanner and figured the little tyke was with you."

"Hopefully the rest of my day will be more relaxed. Oh, one more thing. Would you mind throwing some hay out for the horses? I left in such a hurry, I didn't get a chance to."

"Not at all. Be happy to do it."

"Thanks, Remy." As I hung up, loud protests from my stomach reminded me I hadn't eaten yet either, so I threw the Explorer into drive and headed for the Wagon Wheel Café.

Approaching Cedarville from the south and with less than an hour of patrol left, my radio picked up some rather unusual traffic. "Medic One, report of a male victim buried under a roof avalanche. Five hundred High Street."

"Well Bubbles, maybe the paramedics could use some help digging that guy out." I turned on my overheads and started for the location. Pulling over next to the park in Cedarville, I was surprised to see Haywire's truck parked nearby, and even more surprised when I recognized the boot sticking out of a huge pile of snow in the middle of the driveway.

"Stay here," I told my canine companion as I climbed out. Some of the neighbors, along with the paramedics, were working on removing the snow, so I grabbed a shovel from the back of my patrol unit and ran across the street to help.

"Anyone see what happened?" I asked, shoveling snow from the top of the pile.

"He was using the snowblower to clear the driveway and next thing I know, he's buried under all this snow," one of the neighbors said.

"So you didn't actually see it happen?"

"Sure didn't." We continued digging until Haywire's entire lower half was exposed.

"I'm not seeing any movement," the female paramedic said. "Hurry up and get his head uncovered." Everyone doubled their efforts and within seconds had the rest of him uncovered. His stocking cap had been knocked off and every orifice of his head had been packed with snow.

As she cleared his airway, Haywire began to cough and sputter and pushed everyone away. "What the hell happened?" he demanded. "And what are you all gaping at?"

"With all this melting, looks like the snow slid off the carport and onto you," another neighbor said. "You know, that happened to my sister's brother-in-law. He was trying to knock down icicles and..."

While she continued her story, I stepped away and inspected the carport. With its flat roof, I doubted any snow would have come down without help. Looking around, I located a ladder and climbed up to take a look. A few clumps of snow and a snow shovel lying near the front edge were all that I found. I grabbed it and climbed back down. "Have you been up on the carport shoveling snow?" I asked Haywire.

The others had managed to get him up, and he was sitting on the large scoop of the snowblower. "Hell no!" he replied.

I held up the shovel. "Well, someone has."

"Wondered where that'd gotten to," he said.

"And, it looks like they moved all the snow into one big pile before shoving it off on you."

"Why would someone want to do that?" the woman whose sister's brother-in-law had also been buried in snow asked, but no one offered a theory.

"I think we should take you to the hospital and get you checked out," the other paramedic said. He was very tall and very thin.

"I ain't going to no hospital." Haywire struggled to his feet. "Been spending way too much time there anyway, so you two might as well git," he said, turning to the paramedics.

"We'll need to have you sign a release," the female paramedic said.

"I'll sign whatever you want just so you'll leave me in peace."

She walked over to the ambulance and returned with a clipboard and a pen. After getting the required signature, the two of them packed up their equipment and drove away.

"You sure you're all right?" I asked Haywire.

"I'm fine, 'cepting for all this here snow. Sal's gonna give me what for if she gets home and sees all this."

"Don't you worry about that," the first neighbor said. "We'll all pitch in and help get your driveway cleared, won't we." The rest of the neighbors nodded in agreement. "Won't take us any time at all. You just go on inside and rest and leave it to us."

"Much obliged," Haywire said. "You folks are good neighbors."

I followed Haywire inside and the first thing he did was grab his Colt .45 and stick it into the waistband of his pants. "Is that absolutely necessary?" I asked.

"There's some asshole out there that's got it in for me, and I aim to protect myself."

"I agree there's been some questionable things going on but..."

"Questionable? Cut brake lines and being buried under snow is questionable? I'd say more like lethal. I haven't lived this long just standing around to see what's gonna happen. I'm done being somebody's damn target."

He had a point. "Then may I suggest holding up here for a few days. Keep a low profile and not give this person any more opportunities to finish what they've seemed to have started."

"Exactly what I intend to do." He sat down on the couch, pulled out his gun and laid it across his lap.

"I'll try to drive by here more frequently as I patrol," I began as I headed for the door, "and see if I notice anyone suspicious hanging around."

"Much obliged."

Back at my patrol unit, I let Bubbles out for a pee break. As he shopped around for the best spot to do his business, I nonchalantly looked around but didn't notice anything or anyone out of place. Given Haywire's current state of mind, I decided to stop at the café on the way home and give Sal a heads-up on the situation. Didn't need her bursting into the house unannounced.

CHAPTER 17

When I pushed through the front door of the Sheriff's Office the next day, I was surprised to see Ira sitting at the dispatcher's desk. "Hey Ira," I said. "What's going on?"

"Not much. Slow day so far."

"Where's Cindy?"

"She took the morning off," he replied. "Supposed to be in around eleven. Surprised to see you here so early. How was the trip over the pass?"

"Nothing like last week. In fact, a lot of the snow has melted, leaving bare pavement for most of the way."

"Whatcha got there?" He nodded at the ice chest I was holding.

"Samples for Josh. Intended to bring them in yesterday but..."

"So how did that turn out, by the way?"

"Definitely a happy ending. Located the woman and the baby; everybody is just fine. The owner of the resort even offered them a place to stay until their truck is ready to go."

"Totally awesome," Ira said.

"Agreed. Well, I'm gonna get going before Sandusky spots me. See ya later, Ira."

"Yeah, later Sarah."

"Hey Josh," I said as I entered the lab. "How's my favorite tech?"

"Beings as how I'm the only tech…" He removed the magnifying visor that gave him googly eyes and placed it on the large examining table. "To what do I owe the pleasure of your visit today?"

"More blood samples." I opened the ice chest and removed the two swab boxes.

"Oh?"

"Just following up on a hunch. All I need to know is whether or not they match the ones I brought in the other day."

"Gotcha," he said, reaching for them.

"And is there any way to put a rush on it?"

"I can ask but no guarantees."

"Understood. Thanks." I left the lab, walked partway back up the hallway and swung into the conference room. Given all that had happened since Haywire's initial attack, I figured it was a good idea to write a detailed report in case an actual arrest was made. Choosing a computer out of view of anyone passing by, I turned it on and got started. It took almost 45 minutes and reading through my notebook at least a dozen times, but when I was finished, I had a thorough report detailing all four incidents involving Haywire as well as his truck. I saved it to my flash drive, waved to Ira on my way out and headed back over the pass.

It was nearly ten o'clock when I reached the summit and began my descent toward Surprise Valley. I'd just passed the ski area when a call came over the radio.

"Medic One and Engine 5450, smell of gas and unresponsive male at 500 High Street, cross of Bonner."

Not Haywire again! I stomped on the accelerator and turned on my overheads.

"Unit 113, Modoc."

I grabbed my mic from the dash. "Go ahead, Modoc."

"Got a report of hazardous conditions at 500 High Street."

"Copy. I'm 10-19." I replaced the mic and sped down the hill. Ten minutes later I made a right hand turn onto High Street. Flashing lights from the ambulance that had been there the day before mingled with those on the local fire engine, and a cluster of neighbors had gathered at the end of the driveway. I again pulled in alongside the park and headed toward the front door.

As I stepped inside, the first thing I noticed was Haywire sitting on the couch, wearing an oxygen mask and being tended by the same paramedics from yesterday. All the windows and doors had been flung wide open, and several firemen were moving through the house. Sal noticed me and immediately came over.

"Oh Hon, this is just terrible!" she exclaimed. "It's so lucky I came home when I did."

"What exactly happened here, Sal?" I asked.

"Well, I came home to check on things before the lunch rush and found the place full of propane. Poor Henry was laying on the couch, unconscious. I dialed 911 and opened up the house. They showed up a few minutes later," she said, pointing at the firemen, "and discovered it was the stove."

One of the firemen whose helmet identified him as the chief stepped over to us. "Looks like a burner had been turned on but wasn't lit. Lucky that monitor heater didn't kick on," he said pointing at the small unit on the west wall of the living room, "or this could've been much worse. One of my guys turned it off the second we got here." He paused long enough to wave through a fireman who'd appeared at the door, carrying a large exhaust fan. "It will take a little while for all the gas to dissipate but that should help."

"And I said, I ain't going to no hospital." Haywire pulled the oxygen mask off his face.

"Sir," the female paramedic said, "you need to keep this on." She took the mask and attempted to put it back into place.

"Now, Henry," Sal said, moving over closer to him. "You should listen to these people. They're only trying to help you."

"Don't need no help," he said, pushing the paramedic's hands away. "I'm just fine."

"Tell you what Haywire," I said, "you keep that oxygen on a little while longer and give me a chance to look around a bit. Maybe figure out how this happened."

"Fine." He grabbed the mask and shoved it against his face.

I walked out the front door and started around toward the backyard. A tall, wooden fence ran from the corner of the carport and continued around the perimeter of the property. As I made my way along the back of the house, I watched for any indication someone had been around, but the snow had not been disturbed except where it had been swept off the tiny porch at the backdoor. I continued along the side of the house past what I assumed was the bathroom window until I reached a larger window toward the front of the house where the garage was located. The screen had been removed, and it was wide open. Several footprints indicated travel to and from that area, and I spotted where the individual had climbed over a locked gate.

"Have any of your men been in the garage?" I asked the fire chief when I returned to the living room.

"Don't think so." He turned to the other firemen. "Anybody go into the garage?"

All but one shook their heads. "I didn't go in. Just

opened the door, saw that the window was already open and closed the door again," he said.

"Sal, do you usually keep the window in the garage locked?" I asked.

"Well, actually the lock is broken."

"How about the door into the garage? Do you keep that locked?"

"Not usually. Didn't really see any need to. I know all the neighbors."

"Well, there are footprints outside that window, and a few clumps of snow tracked across the floor of the garage. My guess is that whoever it was might have still been inside the house when you drove up."

"What do you mean inside the house?" Sal asked, sinking down into the nearest chair.

Haywire pulled the oxygen mask off of his face again. "You mean that asshole got in here?"

"That's probably who turned on the gas. What's the last thing you remember?" I asked.

"Well, I was sitting right here reading the paper."

"Do you remember hearing anything?"

"No. Must've dozed off."

I turned to the fire chief. "How long would it take for someone to be rendered unconscious from breathing propane?"

"Well, the house could be filled with the stuff in 15 to 20 minutes. After that, it would depend on the person's age and health condition."

"Why would someone want Henry unconscious?" Sal asked.

"Whoever this is, they searched the cabin up at the mine and searched his truck. They also tried to incapacitate him by dropping snow on him. Why? What's left to search?"

Sal and Haywire looked at each other. "The house!" she exclaimed.

"Have you checked to see if anything's missing?" I asked.

"Why no. As soon as I found Henry, I called for help and tried to wake him up."

"Maybe we ought to take a look," I suggested.

Sal got up and headed toward the hall. Haywire tried to start after her but the paramedics had him cornered.

"Stay there," I told him, "and put that oxygen mask back on."

He glowered at me like he had at Zach yesterday, but he did as he was told.

Sal was in the back bedroom when I caught up to her. "Would you just look at this mess!"

All the dresser drawers were partway open and their contents hanging out. The closet door was open and all her shoes had been tossed out into a pile. The bedding had been pulled loose and the mattress was askew. Together we went into the guest room where Haywire had been staying. That bed was also disheveled, but nothing else had been touched.

"Your arrival must have interrupted whoever did this," I said.

"But why turn on the gas?" Sal asked.

"I think they were waiting for Haywire to pass out so they could search him, too."

"Oh, poor Henry. What if I hadn't come home when I did?"

"The point is you did, and he's going to be okay."

When we returned to the living room, the firemen had left and the paramedics were packing up their equipment. "His heart rate is better and his blood pressure is good," the female paramedic said. "I'd say follow up with his regular physician but..." She shrugged, picked up the remaining cases off the floor and followed her partner out the door.

"Now what?" Sal asked me.

"Well, the first thing you should do is secure the window in the garage and keep the door into the house locked. And as I said before, I'll try and drive by as often as I can, but I have to cover a large area on my patrol."

"I'll get on that right now," Haywire said. "Sally, you got any plywood out in that garage?"

"There might be a small piece or two. Maybe you should just come to the café with me."

"That sounds like a good idea," I said.

"Well, here's the deal," Haywire began, "I need to keep an eye on things here. Can't just go off and leave the place unprotected. I'll get'er all buttoned up good and tight, and then put on a pot of coffee so I don't doze off again." He started toward the hall. "Sally, come give me a hand with that window before you go back to work."

She looked at me and shrugged "Thanks for your help, Hon."

"Sure thing, Sal. See you later." I climbed into my patrol unit, took out my notebook and jotted down some notes about the incident. Then I started the engine and pulled down to Bonner Street and took a left. I'd just reached County Road 1 when my cell phone rang.

"Murdock."

"Hi, Sarah. It's me."

"Oh hey, Cindy. Are you feeling better?"

"Huh?"

"Well, Ira said you weren't coming in to work until eleven. I just assumed it was because you didn't feel well."

"Oh...no. I'm fine. I just needed some time...are you by any chance coming into the office today?"

"Actually I was there this morning. I brought Josh some more blood samples and…"

"More blood samples? Why? What happened?"

A car pulled up behind me, and I waved it by. "Nothing else happened. I'm just following a hunch."

"Oh, I see. Well…"

"Look, is Sandusky there?"

Cindy sighed. "No, he left a little while ago. Had some meeting to go to that should last all day."

I was beginning to understand. The clock on the dash read eleven fifteen. "How about I come back over the hill and grab us some lunch." *Good time to get some work done without running into Dirk the Jerk.* "We can talk in the conference room while I add some stuff to one of my reports."

"That would be great. Thanks."

"See you in awhile." I disconnected and headed for Highway 299. As soon as I reached Alturas, I drove down Main Street to the Burger Pitt and, figuring we both could use some comfort food, ordered two bacon cheeseburgers, two large fries, and two chocolate malts. "Lunch is served," I said as I passed Cindy's desk twenty minutes later. "Follow me."

"Oh my," Cindy said when she came in and saw what I'd ordered. "That's a lot of food."

"Well, if you don't want it…" I reached out as if I was going to take back her share.

She quickly dropped into the chair in front of it and swatted at my hand. "I said nothing of the kind!"

Neither of us had anything to say until most of our burgers and fries were gone. Stirring my malt with the straw I asked, "So what did you want to talk about?"

Cindy pushed what was left of her lunch aside, placed both arms on the table and looked at me. "Dirk."

"I see. Has he been bugging you, trying to make up for shouting at you?"

"That's just it," she said, shaking her head. "He hasn't said a thing."

"Not even an apology?"

"Nothing. Just this tension between us."

"Well..." The radio at the dispatcher's desk interrupted me. Apparently, Cindy had turned up the volume so she could hear it in the conference room.

"Modoc, Unit 125."

Cindy jumped to her feet. "Hang on, I'll be right back." She rushed out of the conference room. "Go ahead, 125. This is Modoc."

"I'm Code 7 at Captain Jack's."

"Copy, 125. Code 7."

"What's Scott doing clear over in Newell?" I asked Cindy when she returned.

"Joe's on vacation, so Scott is covering his patrol along Highway 139."

"That explains why I haven't seen him hanging around in the break room." *Stuffing Pink Snowballs or some other vending machine delicacy into his mouth.*

"What were you going to say?" Cindy asked, swirling one of her fries in a glob of ketchup.

"Maybe he was trying to be something he's not."

"What do you mean?"

"Remember I told you that when people share a traumatic event, they think they have feelings for each other that aren't necessarily true?"

"Yeah, but I told you it wasn't like that."

"Maybe for you it wasn't. But maybe it was different for Sandusky, and he felt...or thought he felt...something for you."

"Then why not say something."

"You said you got to know things about him that explained why he's the way he is. You tell me."

She sat staring at the table for a few minutes. "His ego," she said at last.

"Exactly. He's embarrassed that he might have been confused about his feelings for you, embarrassed that he yelled at you. I'm pretty sure he's embarrassed about not getting into the FBI, and so it's safer in his own mind to treat me like the enemy."

Cindy took a sip of her malt. "You know, I think you may be right. The only thing is..." She paused.

"What's that?" I popped the last bite of my burger into my mouth.

"Christmas is less than ten days away, and we were supposed to spend the holiday together on the coast. I've already told my family I won't be here."

"Come to my house for Christmas. It's just going to be me and Pete, and Remy said he and Shellie might join us."

"That would be great." She picked up her burger and devoured what was left in two bites. "Remember that herd of cowboys you interviewed in October?" she asked as she finished chewing the last bite.

"Yes."

"Did you by any chance get their contact information?" She grinned at me. "Specifically, that tall one with the magnificent, black handlebar mustache."

And she's back! "I might have that tucked away somewhere," I said.

"Perfect!"

"Modoc, Unit 104."

"Oh, gotta go." She jumped to her feet again. "Thanks for lunch."

"Welcome. And as far as Sandusky's concerned..."

159

"Not to worry. I got this." And she dashed through the door.

I disposed of the trash in the break room garbage can and returned to the conference room where I fired up the closest computer, inserted my flash drive, and opened my most recent report. After adding today's incident to it and following a gut instinct (or what a previous boss, and yes I'm sorry to say former lover turned crazed kidnapper, would've called my woman's intuition—if he wasn't accusing me of PMSing), I added a side note about the eight items I'd heard about or that had been reported missing in the past week. Satisfied that I now had a very thorough report building a strong case against whoever was after Haywire, I again saved it to my flash drive.

Cindy was on the phone when I walked by her desk, so I just waved good-bye and pushed through the reinforced glass door. As I came down out of the Warners into Surprise Valley for the second time that day, I decided to stop by and check on Haywire before finishing my patrol and heading home.

CHAPTER 18

A lmost forty-eight hours of radio silence. No reports of theft, vandalism, and more importantly, bodily injury to Henry "Haywire" Heuson. Whether due to more frequent drive-bys during my patrol or the fact that the perpetrator had moved on, I appreciated the quiet. *This calls for a celebration!* I headed for the Wagon Wheel Café.

Nearly an hour later and stuffed from eating an entire club sandwich and what I'm almost certain was a double helping of potato salad—thanks to Sal, I waddled out to the Ford Explorer to continue my patrol. I'd just reached the southern edge of Cedarville when my radio went off.

"Unit 113, Modoc."

Here we go! I grabbed my mic off the dash and responded. "Go ahead Modoc; this is 113."

"Got a 602 at the new storage place. End of the cul-de-sac just past Rabbit Traxx, cross of Bonner. RP, first of Max, will be waiting in the office."

"Copy. I'm 10-19." I continued south until I found a plowed driveway where I could turn around. Heading back toward town, I turned left onto Bonner Street and drove to the end of it and into the entrance of Moore Roome Storage. The sign above the door read, "Ye Olde Office: Proprietor Maxin Moore," and I half-expected to find the owner dressed as a Minute Man. Instead, the man exiting the building resembled a younger version of Danny DeVito with curly dark hair and matching mustache, wearing Wranglers and a tan jacket. I pulled up next to him and got out.

"Deputy Murdock," I said as a means of introduction. "You must be Max."

"That's right," he said as we shook hands.

"You've got a trespasser?"

"Well actually, I think I have someone living in one of my units."

"Really? Why's that?"

"Come on, and I'll show you." He began walking toward the rows of white buildings. "I was taking advantage of the break in the weather to move as much of the snow I'd piled up as possible," he said as we passed by the first three buildings and a small Bobcat loader parked off to one side. "Then I spotted this." He pointed to a bright yellow extension cord coming around the corner of the last building and disappearing into the first unit. "I double-checked, and this one hasn't been rented yet."

"But it has a lock on it," I said.

"Yeah, but it's not one of mine." He pointed to a rented unit in a nearby building. "We provide these disc locks because they're harder to cut off."

"And because there's a cord running into it, you think someone is actually living in there?"

He nodded.

"Do you have a pair of bolt cutters?" I asked.

"Sure, in the maintenance shed."

"Why don't you go get them, and we'll check this unit out."

While I waited for him to return, I looked around but didn't find any obvious footprints in close proximity to the unit. Walking past the building and toward the back of the property, however, I found some that looked vaguely familiar. Just to make sure, I pulled out my phone but the only photos I'd taken at the Winje place with it were of the bloody fingerprints. Switching to camera, I took a couple photos of the footprints I'd found and walked back to my patrol unit. After pulling the camera out of my evidence case, I located a picture of a footprint and zoomed in. Then I did the same with the picture I'd just taken with my phone. *They're a match!* I quickly put away the camera and met up with Max on the way back to the unit.

"I've got plans to fence the entire perimeter and avoid situations like this," he said as we walked along, "but I have to save up some money first. It took everything I had to build this place."

Upon reaching the unit, Max started to hand over the bolt cutters, but I shook my head. "As the owner, I'm going to have you cut the lock off. And because it's locked from the outside, I doubt anyone is there, but just to be safe, we need to stand off to the side when we raise the door."

"I understand," the owner said.

As he stepped over to the lock, I moved to the left side of the door, released the snap on my holster and drew my weapon. Within seconds, the lock fell to the ground, and Max slid the latch to the open position. I nodded to him, and we slowly raised the door.

Just as I had suspected, no one was inside, but it was very obvious someone was, or had been, living there. A lounger with rusty legs had been set up in the middle of the floor and had a couple sleeping bags spread out on it. A neon green work light, hanging from one of the wall side supports, was plugged into the extension cord along with a small space heater and a phone charger.

"I *knew* these were connected somehow," I muttered.

"Sorry?"

"Huh? Oh, nothing. Just thinking out loud."

Until Pete's motorcycle had been stolen last summer, the only other reported thefts had been jewelry taken by a con artist staying at the local nursing home—all of which had been recovered—and a tractor that was found parked in a different outbuilding on the rancher's property. Thievery just wasn't something that happened in Surprise Valley.

"Don't touch anything," I said, holstering my weapon. "I'll be right back." I sprinted to my patrol unit and grabbed my evidence case from the back. Then I opened the driver's-side door, removed one of my own locks from the console and slipped it into the pocket of my jacket. Returning to the unit, I pulled on a pair of gloves, grabbed my camera and stepped inside. Being careful not to disturb anything, I turned on the light and began taking pictures.

"What a mess!" Max exclaimed, pointing to a pile of discarded food containers and water bottles—some empty and others containing a pale yellow liquid. A piece of dark-colored clothing lay on the ground next to the pile.

As soon as I finished taking pictures, I set my camera down on the make-shift bed and picked up the article of clothing, holding it up for closer inspection. It was a hooded sweatshirt, the area surrounding a ragged-looking hole on the right sleeve just below the shoulder stiff with dried blood. "Would you mind grabbing one of those large paper bags out of my evidence case and opening it?" I folded up the sweatshirt and stuffed it into the bag. "Do you have any kind of cameras set up around here?" I asked, sealing it up.

Max shook his head. "They're on the list, right after the fence."

Next, I grabbed a smaller plastic bag and collected some bloody bandages I'd spotted when I picked up the sweatshirt. "I'll take these items with me," I said as I placed both bags into my case and closed it. "The rest of this stuff can stay here for now." I set my evidence case on the ground outside, stepped around the side of the building and unplugged the extension cord. After rolling it up, I tossed it inside the storage unit along with the lock the owner had cut off. Then I pulled the door back down. "I'm putting one of my own locks on here," I said, pulling it out of my pocket and securing the door. "That way whoever is staying here can't get back in. Do you have a camera on your phone?"

"Yes," Max said.

"Good. Keep an eye out for anyone poking around and take pictures if you can, but don't approach them. I'll get a different rig and come back to do some surveillance." I looked around. "Do you have any kind of lighting here?"

"There are a couple of solar, motion-activated spotlights in each row."

"Well, that should help if anyone shows up." I retrieved my evidence case. "It'll be at least an hour before I return."

"That won't be a problem. I still have lots of clearing to do."

"As soon as I get into position, I'll give you a call. Do you have a card or something with your contact information on it?"

"Sure, back in the office."

While Max went in search of a business card, I secured my evidence case in the back of the Explorer and radioed Cindy that I was 10-98 but planned to return in my own vehicle for some surveillance. As soon as Max and I had exchanged cards, I headed north to Fort Bidwell.

It was a quarter to three when I pulled down my driveway and parked in front of my house. After grabbing my tactical vest and evidence case, I hurried inside, plucked my backpack off the floor of my office as I passed through and dumped everything on the kitchen table. Then I removed my winter duty jacket and transferred my radio to the vest and put it on. Knowing my club sandwich and potato salad would only last so long and without a lot of options to choose from, I slapped together a peanut butter sandwich and tossed it into my backpack along with a couple bottles of water, a package of Pop-Tarts, and the last two apples I had in the fridge. Ready to go, I slipped back into my jacket, slung the backpack over one shoulder and grabbed the evidence case. Last thing, I snagged the blanket off the end of the couch as I headed out the door.

"You're off early," Remy said when he answered his door. He motioned me inside.

"Actually, I have to go back and was wondering if you wouldn't mind keeping Bubbles overnight."

"All night, huh?" He led the way into the kitchen. "Sit down for a spell."

"I can't, Remy. I need to get back to Cedarville and keep an eye on a place that has an apparent trespasser."

"A stakeout?" Remy asked, a huge grin on his face.

"More like surveillance to see if this guy shows up?"

"And if he does?"

"Take him into custody."

"Well then, the way I see it, you're going to need backup."

Of course you do!

"Give me just a few minutes to throw some things together, and I'll be right with you." He grabbed a small soft-sided ice chest out of one of the kitchen cupboards and began filling it with jars and containers out of the fridge.

"But Remy, what about Bubbles and Millie?"

"We'll just bring the critters along for extra body heat."

I knew better than to argue with him. They'd accompanied us on previous adventures, so this was nothing new.

Next he grabbed a plastic storage bag out of the bread box and added it to the ice chest. Then he tossed in a couple of tin cups and matching plates from another cupboard, followed by a handful of eating utensils. Last thing, he pulled the partial roll of paper towels off the holder and threw that in. When he finished loading the ice chest, he filled a thermos with what was in the coffeepot. "Just made this a few minutes ago, I'd hate to waste it." Then he put on a heavy coat and his Elmer Fudd hat. "Come on you two," he said, heading for the door. "I'll grab my binoculars out of my rig. May come in handy." Familiar with the antiquated field glasses I'd used on a previous covert surveillance he'd driven me to, I didn't have the heart to tell him I had my own pair of Carson 10x50 binoculars in the Dooley. Anxious to get going, I loaded the animals while Remy went in search of his binoculars, and within minutes, we were headed for Cedarville.

"So what makes this trespasser so important?" Remy asked as we cruised through Fort Bidwell.

"What do you mean?"

"Well, if this was a typical trespasser, you'd have gathered up whatever belongings you found and secured the place so this person couldn't get back in and call it good. But instead, you're going to wait for him to show up and arrest him, so this must be someone special." When I didn't respond, he continued. "Where is it he's trespassing anyway?"

"The new storage place behind Rabbit Traxx."

"And..."

Glancing at Remy, I wasn't surprised to see he'd crossed his arms over his chest and was staring straight at me. Fairly certain I wouldn't get a moment's peace until I told him my suspicions, I gave in. "Based on what I found in the unit this person has been living in..."

"Someone's actually living in one of them things?" Remy asked.

I nodded. "And I think it's the person that jumped Haywire up at the mine."

"You don't say."

"That's why I need to stake out the storage unit, so I can arrest whoever it is when he shows up."

Remy grinned as he settled back into his seat. "Told you you'd need backup."

Oh brother!

CHAPTER 19

The sun had already disappeared behind the Warner Mountains when we reached Cedarville, leaving the Hays Canyon Range bathed in its golden afterglow. I coasted through the four-way stop as I turned right onto Townsend Street. I turned left just past Rabbit Traxx and drove to the end of the cul-de-sac.

"The unit is in that last building on this side," I told Remy as we cruised by, "but we can't park here. There are no houses, so it's way too obvious." Heading back the way we had come, I turned right onto Bonner Street and right again on Patterson. The only spot on that street where the storage unit was visible was also way too obvious. Continuing around the block, I finally found a spot several yards away from the intersection of Bonner and Patterson, where we had a clear view of the storage place. I shut off the engine, pulled Max's business card out of my pocket and dialed his number.

"Moore Roome Storage."

"Hi, Max. This is Deputy Murdock. I'm back in Cedarville and am in position. Have you noticed anyone coming around?"

"No, nothing. I stayed out clearing snow as long as I could, but it just got too cold. So, unless you need me to stick around, I'm going to head on home and stoke up my wood stove."

"That should be fine. I'll let you know if anyone turns up."

"Okay. Good-bye and good luck."

I hung up and dropped my phone into the cupholder of the console. "Now, all we have to do is wait."

The two animals, who had been actively seeking the best vantage point as we traveled south by moving back and forth across the seat, must have realized we were staying put for a while because they curled up together and were soon fast asleep.

"Any idea what this fella looks like?" Remy asked as he rummaged around in the ice chest sitting between his feet.

"None. But considering what he's been able to do, I'm thinking he must be young and fairly agile." I removed my binoculars from their case and scanned the area around the storage units.

"Coffee?" Remy asked.

"Yes, please."

He removed the top of the thermos and filled the two metal cups he'd set on the console, the aroma of freshly brewed coffee filling the cab. "Here you go," he said, offering me one. I set my binoculars on the dash and took it. After replacing the top on the thermos, he picked up his own cup, and we sat in silence sipping our coffee as the last bit of daylight faded from the sky. When it was completely dark, the outside light next to the door of the office suddenly came on. A moment later, the owner stepped out, locked the door and drove away.

"Is that the only light in the place?" Remy asked.

"Supposedly, there are motion-activated spotlights scattered throughout the buildings that should alert us to anyone walking around." I drained my cup and set it on the dashboard next to my binoculars. "Might as well have something to eat while we wait," I said, reaching into the backpack I'd set on the transmission hump in front of the seat.

"Whatcha got in there?" Remy asked.

"Just a peanut butter sandwich and a couple apples."

"Well, I brought some leftover meatloaf and homemade bread to throw together a couple sandwiches, but if you prefer your peanut butter..."

"Do you have a knife I can use?" I asked, pulling out my sandwich and one of the apples.

Remy handed over one he'd packed and watched as I cut my sandwich up into bite-size pieces and did the same to the apple. He chuckled as I passed it all into the backseat.

"Here you go guys, snacktime."

While Remy set about making our sandwiches, I scanned the area through my binoculars, which was limited to the places illuminated by street lamps and the porch light over the door of the Moore Roome Storage office. All I could hope is that the guy set off the motion-activated lights, alerting us to his presence.

"See anything?" Remy asked, passing over my sandwich oozing with mayo and ketchup.

"Not a thing." I set my binoculars back on the dash, balanced the metal plate on the edge of the console and took a huge bite. "Mmm, this is so good," I mumbled around the mouthful of food.

Remy tore a paper towel off the roll and handed it to me. "I believe you're gonna need this," he chuckled.

"Thanks." I wiped the globs of red and white condiments off my face and took another bite. Suddenly, Bubbles jumped up and began to growl as he looked out the window behind me. "This might be it," I whispered, setting down my sandwich. I checked my mirrors, but it was too dark to see anything in their limited field of vision. "Can you see what Bubbles is growling at?"

Remy twisted to the left as he leaned forward. "About the only thing I can make out is a big tree on the other side of the street. Oh wait, I see something moving out there, and I think whatever or whoever it is might be coming this way."

I placed my hand on the door handle, ready to jump out at a moment's notice, and waited. Bubbles' growling became more intense. My eyes strained, trying to see into the darkness, until finally I detected movement. I was just about to leap out of the vehicle when Remy reached out and took ahold of my arm.

"Hold up there."

I glanced at him.

"Don't blow our cover. It's just someone out walking their dog."

I looked out the window again, and Remy was right. An individual, so bundled up against the cold I could not tell whether they were male or female and holding the leash of a very large black dog, walked by without even looking our way. Remy and I glanced at each other and laughed. "Oh that would have taken some explaining had I wrestled that person to the ground."

"Yes, I believe it would've."

Bubbles continued to growl until the dog and its owner rounded the corner and headed south. Then he circled in the seat a few times and lay back down.

We finished our sandwiches and, while Remy tucked things back into his ice chest, I again scanned the storage place as well as the dimly lit areas surrounding us.

"Anything?" he asked.

"Nothing yet," I said, returning the binoculars to their place on the dash. "Got any more coffee?"

"You bet." He dug out the thermos and poured us each one more cup. "Gotcha a piece of apple pie to go with it, if you'd like."

I flashed on the first time I'd met Remy. He'd shown up on my doorstep the day I moved in, holding an apple pie he'd made from what he claimed were the world's best apples. Turned out, he'd picked them off the trees I now own. "Sounds delicious."

As we enjoyed our dessert and coffee, Bubbles moved over to the window and began growling again. "Now what?" I asked the miniature mutt. Remy and I looked out all the windows but neither of us saw anything. "Come on, Dog. There's nothing there." He ignored me and continued growling. "Go on, lie down and go back to sleep." Finally, he stopped and curled up with Millie.

"It seems to be getting colder in here." The last time I'd been on a stakeout in freezing temperatures was on the east coast more than a year ago with only my wool coat to keep me warm. I reached behind me, pulled my blanket into the front seat and opened it up, offering half of it to Remy. "This should help for a while, but we may have to run the heater if it gets too cold in here."

"Don't forget we have them critters to help keep us warm. One of them curled up in your lap should do the trick."

"I'll keep that in mind."

"The way I figure it, we should keep watch in shifts," Remy offered. "That way we won't risk missing that scallawag."

"Yes, I think that would be a good idea," I agreed. "This could be our only chance of nabbing this guy. Once he realizes we're on to him, he just might disappear for good. So who's going to take first shift?"

"Me. I had me a nap right after lunch, so I'm feeling

pretty frisky. You get yourself some shuteye, and I'll wake you if I spot anything."

"Okay but promise you'll wake me the minute you start getting sleepy," I said as I reclined my seat slightly.

"Sure thing." He reached for his antique binoculars.

"Give these a try," I said, handing over mine. "They let in a little more light."

"Well, alrighty then."

I closed my eyes and listened to him getting comfortable as well as the light snoring coming from the backseat. I must have dropped off because the next thing I knew, I heard one of the doors open, and a bright light shone in my eyes. "What's going on?" I demanded.

Remy had stepped out of the vehicle. "Sorry, didn't mean to wake you. Just giving the critters a pee break."

Unbelievable! I reached up and switched off the dome light, hoping no one had seen it. "Hurry up, you're letting out whatever heat we had."

"Come on, you two. Back inside." Remy climbed in after them and had just shut the door when the light on the maintenance shed, which sat behind the Moore Roome Storage office building, lit up.

"I think we've got him. He must have come in from the other direction." I opened my door and turned to Remy. "You stay here and watch. If I need help, I'll try and flash my Maglite at you."

"You watch yourself," he warned.

I closed the door as quietly as I could and took off running toward the last building where the trespasser's unit was located. As I crossed the intersection, a light on the next building went off. There were only three more rows of buildings, so I knew I had to hurry. *If I can get into position before he reaches his unit, I should be able to take him into custody without any problem.* Another light went off as I reached the end of Bonner Street; the trespasser was still moving toward the last building. Going cross country rather than into the driveway, I reach the corner of that building before the next light went off and knelt down. Drawing my weapon, I waited. Seconds ticked by but no one appeared. *Come on, come on!*

More time passed and still no one came around the corner. Debating my next move, another light went off but this time in the wrong direction. I had no other choice but to go after him. I crossed to the other building and hurried down the side of it toward the center aisle. Halfway there, the motion-activated light on the last building went off, momentarily blinding me. Stumbling along, I reached the corner, peered around the building, and there he was. Sitting in the middle of the aisle with his back to me, he paid no attention as he proceeded to lick his front left paw. That's right, the trespasser was a large grey-striped cat who could care less that he'd tricked me into believing I was in pursuit of my suspect.

In hopes of avoiding another wild goose chase, I holstered my weapon, picked up a handful of snow and threw it at the cat. My snowball missed but was close enough to encourage the feline to move on. A couple more and he scampered off between two buildings on the backside of the storage place, and I headed back to the Dooley.

"What in tarnation happened out there?" Remy asked when I opened the door.

"Cat."

"What?"

I pulled my end of the blanket around me. "It was a cat setting off the lights."

"Well, for the love of..." Remy began and then burst out laughing. "A damn cat."

"Yes, a damn cat," I said, glaring at him. "And I chased it away, so hopefully he won't set the light off again." I turned on my side as best as I could given the confines of my seat. *If we catch this guy now, it'll be a miracle.* "Wake me up in a couple hours."

CHAPTER 20

The young man trudged along in the snow toward his hiding place, hoping that the activity that had driven him away was finished and no one was around. As he traveled down Bonner Street toward the vacant field behind Rabbit Traxx, he noticed a white Ford truck he hadn't seen before parked a couple blocks ahead. Crossing the street, he crept close enough to see two people were sitting inside. Suspicious, he slipped behind a nearby tree and waited until his feet became too cold to bear. Cursing his bad luck, he headed for the only other place he had access to. Curled up on the cold cement floor, he decided it was time to end this and go home. "I'm gonna beat it out of that old man—right after breakfast."

Floating up from a deep sleep, I slowly realized something had awakened me. I opened my eyes and, as I glanced over at Remy, I knew what it was. His head was tipped back and his mouth was agape and as he drew in his next breath, the unmistakable raspy gurgle of a deep snore filled the cab. *Oh brother!*

He'd wakened me up around midnight, and I'd kept an eye out for our trespasser until about three. During that time, I'd gotten chilly and coaxed Bubbles into the front seat. After we got settled under my side of the blanket, I woke Remy to take over the surveillance. He obliged, and

I drifted off to sleep. However, he must have dozed off sometime after that. And now the clock on the dash told me it was just after six. Our stakeout was a bust.

"Hey Remy," I said. "Wake up." The only response I got was a small bleat from Millie who had also joined us in the front seat. I repeated myself three times before my self-appointed partner woke up.

"What's going on?" he asked, rubbing his eyes.

"Not a thing." I picked up Bubbles and tossed him into the backseat along with the blanket.

"So what'll we do now?" Remy asked as Millie climbed up onto the center console and leapt into the seat next to her canine companion.

"At this point, I have no idea." My stomach growled. "Maybe I'll think of something after breakfast." I fired up the Dooley and headed for the Wagon Wheel Café. I pulled in next to a familiar metallic pink Cadillac, and we went inside.

Sal was making the rounds with the coffee pot, so we hustled toward our usual spots, hoping to get a cup before the pot ran dry. We'd just gotten comfortable when Haywire pushed through the door.

"Howdy," he said as he joined us at the counter. "You folks are out and about early."

"Morning," Remy replied.

"I'm surprised to see you," I said. "Thought you were going to stand guard at Sal's place."

"No need. I've got that place buttoned up tighter than Fort Knox, and as for myself..." He pulled back one side of his coat, revealing his Colt .45 resting in a well-worn leather holster.

"Now, Haywire..." I began.

"Save it," he said, dropping his coat back into place. "Unless you plan on arresting me right here, right now,

I'm gonna protect me and what's mine until whoever's got it in for me is long gone."

In hopes of convincing him to disarm, I considered telling him about the possible lead I had but decided it wasn't the correct time or place. Perhaps he'd listen to reason after we'd all had a good breakfast.

With half a pot left, Sal approached the counter and all three of us held out our mugs. "Yeah, yeah," she said as she passed by, "be right with you."

We exchanged glances and then watched as she set down the coffeepot, yanked her purse out from under the cash register, and pulled out her wallet. "Why that little..." She whipped around the end of the counter and hustled back to the table nearest the front door. She spoke to Marjorie Callaghan, who was sitting in the next booth, and then stood as if she were waiting for something. Moments later, a young man came out of the restroom and approached her.

"Excuse me, is this your credit card?" Sal asked, holding it out.

"Uh, yeah it is," he said. As he reached for it, Sal punched him in the stomach, and he folded like a cardboard cutout.

"Like hell it is!" She shoved him to the ground, straddled him, and sat on his chest. Haywire, Remy and I jumped up and rushed over, but before any of us could get there, Sal slapped the young man across the face. "That'll teach you to steal from a lady!"

"Okay, Sal. That's enough," I said as I helped her to her feet. "What exactly is going on?"

"This brazen thief tried to pay for his breakfast with my own credit card!" she exclaimed, waving it at him.

"Are you sure?" I asked.

"Of course I'm sure. As soon as I saw it, I dug my wallet out of my purse and sure enough it was missing."

Haywire grabbed hold of the young man who was just beginning to catch his breath and jerked him to his feet.

"Hey, I know you!" he exclaimed. "Aren't you Benny's nephew?"

"Yeah, that's right," he said, pushing Haywire away.

"Who's Benny?" I asked.

"My bookie in Vegas," Haywire replied.

I turned back to the young man. "What's your name?"

"Elvis," he said, brushing himself off. "Elvis Betts."

"Elvis?" Remy asked, and the young man glared at him.

I noticed a partially healed gash on his forehead. Remembering the hooded sweatshirt I'd found, I glanced at his right arm and spotted the bottom edge of a bandage beneath the sleeve of his T-shirt. "You're the one that's been harassing Haywire, aren't you?" I asked.

No reply.

"And you're also who's been living in that unit over at the Moore Roome Storage," I continued.

"What's it to you?" He crossed his arms in front of his chest.

I turned to Haywire. "Do you want to press charges?"

"Hell, yes I do."

"What do you mean, press charges?" Elvis asked. "It's not my fault that my uncle Bennie told me to get the money back."

"Why would he want the money back?" Haywire demanded. "I won that money fair and square."

"Well, he thinks you cheated somehow and sent me after you, but I never thought I'd end up here freezing my butt off."

"Elvis Betts, you're under arrest for assault and trespassing..."

"What about my stolen credit card?" Sal interjected, waving it at the young man again.

"Did you use Sal's credit card anywhere else?"

"The grocery store."

"That must've been where he lifted it out of my wallet," Sal said. "Last Sunday, I'd grabbed some cash and left it sitting on the front seat of my car. That's the only time it has been out of my sight."

"Well?" I said, turning back to Elvis.

He just stared at me and shrugged his shoulders.

"And fraudulent use of a credit card," I added to the charges. *And vandalism if the DNA on those blood samples match!* I continued to recite the rest of the Miranda Rights as I cuffed his hands behind his back.

"What about my coat?" he said, nodding toward the booth where he'd been sitting.

Sal picked up the dark grey jacket with a fur-lined hood and held it out.

"Check that label," I told her. "I'll be willing to bet it does not have the name Elvis Betts on it."

She turned the jacket so she could see the label. "Why, this belongs to Mike over at Rabbit Traxx."

"And I'm pretty sure he'll appreciate getting it back." I took it and as I tucked the coat under my left arm, I noticed a malodorous aroma coming from it. "Although, he may want to wash it first. Remy, I guess you'll have to wait here while I take Elvis to Alturas and book him."

"I'd be happy to take him home," Haywire offered. "Still owe him for helping get me down off that mountain."

"Well, then that settles it." Remy said. "I'll just come grab those critters for you."

"Critters?" Haywire asked. "What critters?"

"They won't be no bother," Remy added as he headed for the door with Haywire right behind him.

"What critters?" he asked again.

While the two of them discussed the best way to

transport a goat and a small dog, I secured Elvis in the backseat—the second time I'd transported a suspect in my personal vehicle since becoming a deputy—climbed into the driver's seat and radioed dispatch.

"Modoc, Unit 113."

"Go ahead 113."

"I've got a 10-15 and en route to CJ with one. ETA is 40 minutes."

"You got him? Uh, I mean...copy, 113. Time is 6:48."

After a quick stop at Rabbit Traxx to return Mike's coat, I headed over Cedar Pass to book my prisoner into the county jail. At half past seven, I eased through the sally port door, the fenders of my Dooley barely clearing the opening, and waited for the door to roll down behind me before getting out. A female correctional deputy I did not recognize stepped out of the intake area and approached my vehicle. Pepperdine was the name on her uniform.

"Wow, looks like what they say is true," she said.

"How's that?"

She smiled. "You know, the early bird gets the worm."

"Oh yeah, that."

"Were you working undercover?" she asked, nodding at my truck.

"Not exactly. It's a long story. I just happened to be in my personal vehicle when I made the arrest."

"Gotcha. So what do you have for us?"

"Young Caucasian male arrested for trespassing, assault, and fraudulent use of a credit card. No signs of suicide or hostility."

"Ok then, let's get your prisoner inside." She opened the rear door and pulled a laminated index card out of her shirt pocket. It was at that point I realized she was another new hire. "Are you suicidal?" she asked Elvis.

"No."

"Have you ever felt suicidal?"

"No." He looked away. "But I'm pretty sure my uncle is going to kill me," he mumbled.

"Have you been in an accident?"

"No."

"Have you been in an altercation?"

He turned back to look at the deputy. "Does being beaten up by an old lady count?"

Deputy Pepperdine looked at me.

"Part of that long story. I can give you the details when we get inside as well as information on the other injuries he's recovering from.

"Okayyyy. Just one more question," she said, turning back to Elvis. "Do you have any illegal drugs, weapons, or other contraband on your person?"

"No."

"Great. Now, we can go in." She slipped the laminated card back in her pocket and stepped on the running board. Reaching in, she unbuckled his seatbelt, grabbed his upper arm and helped him climb down out of the truck. After she quickly searched him, we escorted him into the intake area and had him sit on a bench that had been bolted to the floor.

While I worked on the necessary paperwork, the medical staff began their evaluation of the prisoner. When questioned about the injuries to his head and right arm, he refused to answer, so I filled them in on the assault charge based on the alleged attack on Haywire which had resulted in the two injuries. With the evaluation completed, I finished up the booking documents and turned Elvis over to be photographed, fingerprinted and placed in a cell.

Once clear of the sally port, I pulled over to the rear entrance of the Sheriff's Office, grabbed my evidence case and went inside. I'd learned early on in my career as deputy that Sheriff Chet Atkins did not like surprises and expected his deputies to keep him informed. I also learned that he did not appreciate jokes about his name—a lesson that Deputy Jenkins learned the hard way when the sheriff caught him in the act. To that end, I decided to fill him in on my current investigation and resulting arrest. Besides, I had evidence to pass on to Josh. As I headed down the hall, the sheriff came out of the staff break room, and we met at the door to his office.

"Good morning, Sir. I was just..."

"Morning, Murdock. Glad you're here. There's something I need to talk to you about." He motioned me inside and closed the door after entering.

Oh, this may not be good.

"Sit down," he instructed as he moved around his desk. The sheriff was not a big man but moved with the confidence of someone much taller. He kept his curly brown hair clipped short and his uniform immaculate. When we both were seated, he began. "Undersheriff Sandusky has lodged a complaint against you..."

Now what?

"...for insubordination and a lack of respect for a superior."

"I can explain..."

He held up his hand. "Look, I know Dirk can be a royal pain in the ass, but he does have a point. Would you call me Atkins?"

"Of course not. You're the sheriff."

"And he's the undersheriff. So in the future, I'd appreciate it—think of it as a personal favor—if you would address him by his proper title."

"Yes, Sir."

"Good. Now, that's all I had to say. Back to work."

"Yes, Sir." I got up and was almost to the door before I remembered why I was there. "By the way," I said turning back to the sheriff, "I just wanted to bring you up to speed on my current investigation."

Ten minutes later, I was opening the door to leave. "Good work," Sheriff Atkins said, "and I'll look into that bookie."

"Thank you, Sir." I pulled the door closed and stepped across the hallway to the lab.

"Hey Sarah," Josh said. "You seem to be making a habit of showing up here first thing in the morning."

"Seems that way, doesn't it." I opened my case, pulled out the evidence I'd collected at the storage place and handed it over. "I need to have this blood evidence processed."

"More blood?"

"Yeah. Just need to know if it matches the other samples."

"Gotcha."

"Thanks." I closed my case and started for the door.

"Oh, hey Sarah. The guys are heading over to Lenny's Bar tonight, and I've got Mom's minivan. Thought maybe you'd like to join in." An enterprising young man, Josh offers his services as a designated driver, charging each passenger for a ride home.

"You still only charging five dollars a head?" I asked.

Josh shook his head. "Took your advice. Twenty bucks a pop and double that if they puke."

"Good for you and thanks for the invite but I've got knitting class tonight."

"Yeah, right. Knitting class." He burst out laughing. "That's a good one, Sarah." Figuring it wasn't worth explaining, I just smiled back, gave him a thumbs up and left.

A little over an hour later, I was back at my place. After removing my tactical vest, I transferred it and my evidence case to my patrol unit and headed inside for a quick shower and hopefully something to eat. A note tacked to the door informed me that Remy had fed the horses and, if I was hungry, to stop by his house on my way back out on patrol. *Good old Remy!*

"Thanks again for making dinner," I said as I followed Remy up the narrow, steep stairway.

"I figured that by the time you got that scallawag where he belonged and put in a day of patrolling you'd be worn out and hungry. Especially after being on a stakeout all night."

Don't remind me! "What about you?"

"Oh, me and the critters had a nice long nap."

Figures!

The moment we walked through the doorway, everyone seated around the large table started clapping. I felt embarrassed, but Remy seemed to stand a little taller, as though the applause were for him by association. We'd barely taken our seats when the questions began.

"I understand the person you arrested was a professional hit man," Herb said.

"Well, actually he was..."

"And that he'd been hired by some big time bookie out of Vegas," Abigail added, cutting me off before I could answer.

"No, you see..."

"Well, I heard he moonlighted as an Elvis impersonator," Eloise said.

"Nonsense," Marjorie said. "I just happened to be there, and he didn't resemble the King of Rock in the least."

"Is it true that Sal's boyfriend is a millionaire?" Mabel asked. "I heard he'd hit it big gambling in Vegas."

"Ladies, ladies," I said, looking around the table. "And Herb." He smiled meekly at me. "The young man was just a kid working for his uncle that got in over his head. And he wasn't an Elvis impersonator, his name was Elvis. And as far as Haywire being a millionaire..." I shook my head.

Shellie leaned closer to Remy. "Why would anyone name their son Elvis?"

He looked at me, and I shrugged. "Maybe his mother had been dating an Elvis impersonator when she got pregnant," I offered.

"Ohhh," the others all said in unison.

"And before you start asking any more questions, I'm not really at liberty to discuss the details. But what I can tell you is that I have located all your missing items."

"You have?" Bonnie said. "How?"

"Stumbled upon them during my investigation, and I'll be returning them to you first thing Monday morning."

"I'll be so glad to get my charger back," Eloise said. "I keep forgetting to take my other one when I volunteer at the library."

"Speaking of volunteering," Herb began, "do any of you know anyone who might be interested in volunteering at the convalescent hospital? We really need people to check on residents and see if they need anything. Perhaps play games or have someone to sit with during mealtime. Some even want help decorating their rooms or putting things away."

"Decorating their rooms?" Abigail asked.

"Well, yes. New residents might want to have things arranged a certain way. And almost everyone likes to have holiday decorations put up."

"Well, that's right up my alley. I love working on

interior design and since we've finished refurbishing the resort..."

I flashed on the entryway of the High Desert Hot Springs with its huge ferns, brass furniture with white cushions, large floral prints hanging on the walls and the giant chess set with two-foot playing pieces.

"...I've actually missed it."

"Does that mean you're interested?" Herb asked.

"Well sure, why not," Abigail said. "Ed is not going to believe this."

As other conversations started up around the table, Remy leaned closer and whispered, "Are you sure you can just return all those things?"

"With all the other charges against Elvis, I figured we could overlook the petty theft, especially since all the stolen items had been recovered in relatively good shape."

"Well, alrighty then," he said, pulling his own knitting from the large bag that had previously belonged to his wife. "Oh, I almost forgot to tell you about Haywire's money?"

"What about his money?"

"You'll never guess where he ended up stashing it so that scallawag wouldn't find it."

I waited for him to continue and when he didn't I asked, "Where?"

"In the drum of the swamp cooler hanging on the back of the house."

"But I walked around back there and didn't see any sign of footprints around there."

"Apparently, he edged his way along the side of the house where there wasn't any snow and lifted out one of the side panels without disturbing the snow on top. By the time he got done, you couldn't tell anyone had been there."

"Huh," I said. *Not sure I would have thought of that.*

"Looks like you didn't get much practice in," Robin said as she came around the table toward me.

I looked at the bare needles protruding from the ball of brown yarn. "Well, it's been a rather hectic week, you see, what with a snow rescue and..." Suddenly, I remembered something. "So Abigail, did that couple get to continue on their journey?"

"Why yes they did, Dear," she said. "Left first thing Tuesday morning with the correct directions to get to Burns, Oregon in plenty of time for Christmas."

"That's wonderful. Oh, Christmas—Remy, remind me to tell you something. Okay," I said, turning back to Robin, "time to practice." I quickly made a slipknot and cast on several stitches and then paused. *Now what?*

Noticing my hesitancy, Robin said, "Under, around."

I glanced around and saw Remy making the same motion over and over again with his knitting needles, like he was stuck in a loop video. Finally, I realized he was trying to show me what to do, so I copied him with my own needles.

"Good," Robin said. "Now slide left into the loop, push up and off."

Again, Remy demonstrated and I copied him.

"Great," Robin said, sliding onto the table between us and blocking my view of Remy. "Do another one."

Dammit!

"Under, around," she said, and I began the stitch. "Slide left into the loop, push up and off." I finished the stitch, and Robin laughed as she got up. "Keep going," she said, "and maybe now that you've caught the bad guy, you can actually practice." I smiled at her and continued adding stitches until I got to the end of the first row.

"What did you want to tell me?" Remy asked after I'd switched needles and was about to start the second row.

"Huh?"

"A couple minutes ago, you said you had something to tell me."

I stared at him for a few seconds before it came to me. *Christmas!* "Oh, yeah. So Cindy has called it quits with Sandusky and..."

"Good for her!"

"...and I invited her to spend Christmas at my house. You don't mind do you?"

He smiled. "Hell's bells why should I mind. The more the merrier."

"Great!" I continued to add stitches and had completed several rows when my phone vibrated. Thinking it might be a text from Cindy, I pulled it out of the front pocket of my jeans. It was a text all right but not from Cindy.

"Something the matter?" Remy asked. "You look like someone done punched you in the stomach."

"My mom just texted me. Looks like she and my dad are coming for Christmas."

"Well, won't that be nice."

"Yeah, won't it," I said. "But I doubt it," I mumbled, shoving my phone back into my pocket. My mother always went a little overboard at Christmas with decorating and cooking special meals, and I doubted this one would be much different other than it all would be happening at my house.

"I've been looking forward to meeting them and..." He suddenly stopped and turned to me, the look on his face a cross between agony and panic.

"Something wrong?" I asked.

"That sister of yours ain't coming is she? Because if she shows up, you can count me out."

You and me both! I chuckled. "No Remy, my sister isn't coming."

"Well, alrighty then—if you're sure."

"My sister doesn't come home for Christmas. She prefers somewhere more exciting." As I continued knitting, something kept bothering me, but I couldn't quite figure out what. Finally, I pulled out my phone and re-read my mother's text. The first part of it was the usual update of what she and my father had been doing, then she talked about some kind of arrangements having to be made, but it was the last line that got my attention. "...and so all of us are coming for Christmas." *Oh please, someone—anyone—give me a break!*

Shoving my phone into my pocket again, I realized Remy was watching me. "All good," I said, offering a dubious smile. *That is, until you find out who's coming to Christmas dinner!*

Made in the USA
Las Vegas, NV
21 April 2023

70930846R00121